FIRE
IN THE
GATES

FIRE
IN THE
GATES

The Story of Baruch, Jeremiah, and Nebuchadnezzar

THURMAN C. PETTY, JR.

REVIEW AND HERALD® PUBLISHING ASSOCIATION
Since 1861 | www.reviewandherald.com

Cover design by Trent Truman
Cover art by Thiago Lobo

Printed by Pacific Press® Publishing Association

The author assumes full responsibility for the accuracy of all facts and quotations as cited in this book.

Additional copies of this book can be obtained by calling toll-free 1-800-765-6955 or by visiting http://www.adventistbookcenter.com.

Library of Congress Cataloging-in-Publication Data
Petty, Thurman C., 1940–
  Fire in the gates : the drama of Jeremiah and the fall of Judah / Thurman C. Petty, Jr.
     p. cm.
  ISBN 978-0-8127-0443-3
 1. Jeremiah (Biblical prophet)—Fiction. 2. Bible. O.T.—History of Biblical events—Fiction. I. Title.
  PS3566.E894F57 2007
  813'.54—dc22
                    2006102909

November 2016

Dedication

To my wife, Martha,
who supported me in many ways
while I wrote this manuscript;

and to my son Joel and my daughter Esther,
who love Bible stories.

Contents

A Chronology of Jeremiah's Time

Years BC	Babylon	Judah	Prophets	Major Events
627				
626	+			
625				
624			Jeremiah	
623				
622				
621				
620				
619				
618		Josiah		
617				
616	Nabopolassar			
615				
614				
613				Fall of Nineveh
612				
611				
610				
609				
608				
607				
606				
605				Jerusalem: First Captivity
604				
603		Jehoiakim		
602			Daniel	
601				
600				
599		+		
598		Jehoiachin		Jerusalem: Second Captivity
597		+		
596				
595				
594	Nebuchadnezzar			
593				
592				
591		Zedekiah	Ezekiel	
590				
589				
588				
587				
586		+		
585				Jerusalem Destroyed
584				
583				
582			=*	
581			=	
580				

*Date for the end of Jeremiah's ministry not known

9

Jerusalem in the Time of Jeremiah

(compiled by Thurman C. Petty, Jr., from several maps.)

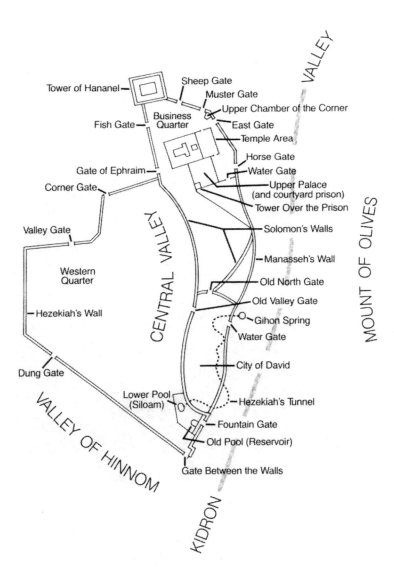

- VALLEY
- Sheep Gate
- Tower of Hananel
- Muster Gate
- Upper Chamber of the Corner
- Business Quarter
- Fish Gate
- East Gate
- Temple Area
- Horse Gate
- Gate of Ephraim
- Water Gate
- Upper Palace (and courtyard prison)
- Corner Gate
- Tower Over the Prison
- Solomon's Walls
- Valley Gate
- CENTRAL VALLEY
- Manasseh's Wall
- MOUNT OF OLIVES
- Western Quarter
- Old North Gate
- Old Valley Gate
- Hezekiah's Wall
- Gihon Spring
- Water Gate
- City of David
- Dung Gate
- Lower Pool (Siloam)
- Hezekiah's Tunnel
- Fountain Gate
- VALLEY OF HINNOM
- Old Pool (Reservoir)
- Gate Between the Walls
- KIDRON

Chapter 1

Murder Plot at Anathoth

"You've troubled us for the last time," Pashur growled as he grabbed Jeremiah by the arm. "Come with us." Pashur's son Gedaliah helped him drag the prophet toward the middle of the prison courtyard. "You're going to have a fatal accident, and then we'll see what becomes of your prophecies!"

Although Jeremiah struggled to free himself, their strength exceeded his. "What are you doing?" he gasped as they neared the cistern and he noticed that someone had removed its lid.

"Too bad you're not watching where you're going, Jeremiah," Pashur laughed. "No one will likely find you down there."

"No!" Jeremiah protested. "You can't do this. I'll die down there."

"That would be dreadful," Gedaliah smirked as he and his father tied a rope under Jeremiah's armpits and shoved the prophet into the dark hole.

"Stop!" the prophet screamed as he fought to grip the sides of the opening. But Pashur stamped on his fingers, and he had to let go. The rope bit into his underarms, burning and bruising the skin. He found the cistern deeper than he had imagined, and when he reached the bottom, he sank up to his armpits into slimy, frigid mud and water.

Desperately Jeremiah shouted until his voice grew hoarse, but no one could hear him. In spite of his sore fingers, he hadn't been seriously hurt, but the cold mud chilled him to the bone. Numbly, he tried to comprehend his peril, as he stood in the watery muck. Even if he extracted himself from the slippery mess, he couldn't see the cistern's opening in the darkness, let alone reach it. And even if he could, he would be too weak to push the covering out of the way by himself.

His fingers throbbed. *If no one rescues me soon, I'll die!* In his desperation, he prayed, "Oh, Yahweh,★ please save me!"

His mind drifted, and he began to think about the amazing journey on which God had taken him during his life. He recalled when God had first summoned him to be a prophet and the long journeys he had taken in his early ministry as he encouraged his people to worship their Creator once more.

During his first preaching tour he'd visited every city and village in Judah. How tired and hungry he had been when he finally neared home again after so many months away. In his mind he could still see the road and the trees and hear the songs of the birds. A voice in the distance called his name.

"Jeremiah! Jeremiah!" the young man jogging up the road from Anathoth shouted.

"What is it, Baruch?" Jeremiah quickened his steps. "Why do you run?" He abruptly halted when he saw the terror in his friend's eyes. "What's the matter?"

"Your uncles—they've vowed to kill you!" Baruch puffed to a stop, as pearls of sweat trickled into his beard.

"Kill me?" The prophet's face paled. "But why?"

"They don't like your preaching. I've heard that they're watching every gate in town to catch you when you enter. I wanted to stop you before they got you."

"But why?"

"I don't know, Jeremiah, but you can't come home."

★ Yahweh, the Hebrew name for God, has been translated Jehovah, or the Lord, in older English versions of the Bible.

Baruch glanced around. His gaze fell on the city walls three miles down the valley. "The road to Jerusalem lies around the next bend—you could reach it before dark."

"I guess that's what I'll do," Jeremiah sighed after a moment. For a moment a longing for Anathoth, his boyhood home, swept over him. "Yahweh warned me about this. In spite of King Josiah's reforms, our people still hate the truth about them and the prophets who preach it."

"Yes, Jeremiah." Baruch squeezed his friend's arm. "But you'd better go. It's nearly sunset, and we shouldn't be seen together."

"You're right." Following ancient custom, Jeremiah kissed Baruch goodbye on both cheeks. "Come see me when you can."

By the time Jeremiah rounded the bend on his way toward Jerusalem, Baruch had already disappeared. Soon the prophet from Anathotz studied the stone walls in the distance, to the right of the Mount of Olives. "Where will I live in Jerusalem?" Jeremiah repeated to himself in time with his steps.

Jeremiah mentally reviewed the situation. Josiah had died fighting Egypt. God had shown the prophet that Pharaoh Necho would soon capture King Jehoahaz, Josiah's son, and hold him hostage in Egypt. As for Jeremiah himself, now his own kinfolk plotted to kill him. "O, Yahweh," he prayed aloud, "have You deserted us? I know that the people worship in the Temple and call upon Your name merely out of superstition, and even the priests regard the worship service as a magical rite. But can't You do something?"

The sky glowed crimson behind Jerusalem as Jeremiah strode through the Sheep Gate. He scarcely noticed the stench of raw sewage rising from the poorly covered conduit that passed through the gate, as it did in every walled town in Judah. As he entered, an old man rose from a bench just inside the city gate and turned toward his home. Otherwise the cobblestone streets lay deserted.

Where can I find a room? Jeremiah wondered as he stood on aching feet inside the gate. A rumbling from behind startled him, and he turned to see the guards closing the giant cedar doors. "I made it just in time," he said to one of them.

"You did, at that," the man returned without looking Jeremiah's direction. Then he bounded up the steep stone steps to the top of the wall and disappeared.

The homeless prophet started down the empty streets. Ahead lay the merchant's quarter, and Jeremiah knew that he would find little help there at this time of day. To his right an avenue passed the tower of Hananel, bent to the left toward the Fish Gate, around the west end of the Temple complex, and extended into the Western Quarter—the newest part of Jerusalem—comprised mostly of homes. "Perhaps I'll go that way," he mumbled as he shuffled to the right, glancing at the doors on both sides of the street.

Voices echoed down from windows overlooking the avenue and mingled with the lowing of cattle, the bleating of sheep, and the braying of donkeys coming from the stalls on the first floors of most homes.

He'd walked for half an hour when, in the dim light, he spotted the symbol of the high priest on one door. "That's it!" he whispered, pounding his right fist into his left palm. "I'm a priest. The Temple steward should help me."

Revived feet scurried back toward the Temple and the steward's house nearby. *That official supplies the needs of all the priests,* Jeremiah reasoned. *Why didn't I think of him before?*

After rapping his calloused knuckles on the plank door, Jeremiah soon heard the thumping of feet descending the steps from the living quarters upstairs. The speakinghole cover flipped open with a whack, and a man growled, "What do you want?"

"I'm Jeremiah from Anathoth." His voice sounded tired. "I need somewhere to sleep and something to eat."

"So? Why bother me?"

"Because I'm a priest and you're the steward." *Not to mention that you're supposed to give hospitality to a stranger,* Jeremiah thought to himself.

"A priest, eh?" The man's tone softened a little. "Yes, you did say Anathoth, the priests' village."

"Yes, sir."

"Well, go home, then—it's not far."

"They put me out, sir."

"Oh. Well—all right." The hinges creaked as the steward opened the door and sighed. "But we'll find you another place tomorrow."

Jeremiah stepped inside, waited for his host to bar the door, and followed him up a flight of stairs. The steward placed an olive oil lamp on a ledge in a musty room that lacked both ventilation and furniture. "The wife will bring you a mat and porridge," he muttered as he closed the door.

The squat woman who delivered the food was as taciturn as her husband. Jeremiah pitied the pair. They had the means and opportunity to bless their fellow Levites, but they did only what custom required—nothing more.

Jeremiah drank the warm, watery soup, lay down on the mat, and drowned in his own thoughts. The king's death and his own exile blended with the soup and the bare room, tumbling over in his mind. Once he thought Baruch entered with the steward and his stooped wife, but when Jeremiah tried to touch his friend, the man vanished.

Suddenly Jeremiah sat up. Morning! "Just a bad dream," he muttered. But no. The bare room, the thin sleeping mat, the empty bowl, and the sound of angry voices from below reminded him that his nightmare was real.

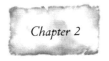

Chapter 2

A Goblet of Wine

"Where do the Rechabites live?" Jeremiah asked a young woman who balanced a full water jar on her head. She breathed heavily, for she had climbed nearly 300 feet in her half mile trek up from the Pool of Siloam. Jeremiah guessed that she lived near the Valley Gate—she had another 100 feet to climb before she reached home.

The woman stopped and studied the man who had spoken. He stood taller than most, had blue-black hair, hazel eyes, swarthy skin, and his bushy beard sported flecks of gray. His ankle-length, close-fitting, white-linen garment marked him as a priest.

"I think they live near the tower of Hananel," she finally answered. "Lots of them over there."

"Thank you, woman. May Yahweh bless you."

"Don't speak of Yahweh to me!" she hissed, nearly dropping her water jar. "Ashtoreth rules now. She's the queen of heaven." Then she spit on the ground to show her disgust and strutted off.

"If I asked a dozen people which god they worshipped, I'd get a dozen different answers," Jeremiah mused aloud as he followed her directions. He trudged through a short, dim alley where the owners of houses on both sides of the street had built adjoining rooms over the walkway. The avenue widened, curved to the left near the Corner Gate, and descended several stone steps into the potter's section of Jerusalem. Momentarily Jeremiah paused to watch an artisan fashion a clay vessel on his wheel.

Turning northward near the Ephraim Gate, Jeremiah passed behind the Temple complex and into the merchant's quarter near the Fish Gate. As he neared the tower of Hananel he asked an old man about the Rechabites.

"Some live on the next street, in the shadow of the tower." The stoop-shouldered man pointed with his walking stick. "You'll find them at most any house."

"May Yahweh bless you, sir," Jeremiah said.

"Why, thank you, son." The old man smiled. "I'd forgotten to recite that phrase today. Be bad luck if I didn't say it at least once."

Bad luck! Jeremiah recoiled as he left the man. *He thinks of Yahweh as a good-luck charm.*

The prophet cut through a narrow passage between houses to reach the next street, turned right, and knocked on the first door. "I'm looking for Jaazaniah," he announced.

"That's my husband!" The startled woman stepped back. "What do you want with him?"

"A matter of sacred business." Jeremiah smiled.

The woman studied his face, then relaxed. "Do come in," she said, stepping aside. "He will return soon." She swung her hand toward a stool, disappeared into another room, and quickly returned with a cup of water.

As Jeremiah sipped the last drops from his goblet, Jaazaniah entered. "I'm Jeremiah," he said, rising from the stool. "I have important business with you and the other Rechabites at the Temple."

Jaazaniah nodded and retreated back out the door, returning moments later with several relatives.

"Come with me," Jeremiah said as he led the group toward the Temple, saying nothing about his mission. He guessed they would refuse to go with him if they knew what lay ahead.

The group entered a small room near the eastern wall,

attracting a considerable crowd in the process. Jeremiah motioned to the men to gather around the large table set with several earthenware pitchers and goblets. Grasping a pitcher, he poured some of its liquid into a goblet and extended it toward the Rechabite leader. "You've been a good man, Jaazaniah—you deserve the best. Have a drink of Judah's finest wine."

"No!" Both hands shielding himself from the cup in Jeremiah's hand, Jaazaniah backed away. "I mean—" He seemed embarrassed as he realized that Jeremiah might misunderstand his actions. "Thank you, sir, but I don't drink wine."

The mumble of voices beyond the open door reminded the group that a crowd stood out in the courtyard.

"Why not?" Jeremiah pressed, his face showing concern.

"Because, many years ago our father, Jonadab, the son of Rechab, commanded us never to drink wine or live in any dwelling besides a tent. We have always obeyed him. We've drunk no wine all these years, and lived in tents until the Babylonians drove us into Jerusalem." He straightened his shoulders. "Thank you for your thoughtfulness, but we cannot drink your wine."

Jeremiah smiled at him, set the goblet down, and headed toward the door. "You may wonder what this is all about," he said to the crowd. "The Rechabites refuse to drink my wine because one of their ancestors forbade it."

Smiles crossed many faces, for all respected ancient traditions.

Then Jeremiah began to shout so that all could hear. "The Rechabites obey their earthly father, but you all disobey your heavenly Father. Yahweh has sent many prophets to you, warning you to repent, but you have refused to listen." The sudden change of mood caught them by surprise. "My people," he pleaded, "unless you repent, Yahweh will destroy this city!"

Turning to the Rechabites, he said, "Because you have obeyed your father, you will receive God's blessing forever." Then slipping through a door into an adjoining room, Jeremiah disappeared.

Chapter 3

Riot in the Temple

The slopes of the Mount of Olives sprouted tents and brush shelters as pilgrims prepared for the Feast of Tabernacles. Women gossiped around their cooking fires, men gathered in small circles to exchange tales or bits of news, and children chased each other or played a chesslike game called "hounds and jackals." Few recalled that the feast commemorated Israel's 40 years of wilderness wanderings—most regarded it as merely another holiday. As the hour for the grand procession arrived, everyone clambered up the Kidron Valley Way toward the East Gate, each carrying his handwoven palm or willow branch fronds.

Jeremiah joined the procession inside the Temple gate as the multitude sang psalms while they waved their fronds. They crossed the outer court and entered the inner court, and while the priests marched around the altar, the women moved to one side and the men to the other.

The high priest raised his hands over his head, and the tumult died. A middle-aged priest stepped forward to speak, but no one heard him, for another voice bellowed from back in the crowd.

"Hear the words of Yahweh." Jeremiah stood on a stone bench at the gateway between the two courts. "You treat Yahweh's Temple as though it were a magical charm when you say, 'the Temple of the Lord, the Temple of the Lord,' but what good is your worship when you refuse to love your neighbors?

"This Temple bears Yahweh's name, but it will not last forever. The tabernacle at Shiloh also bore His name, but it passed away. Unless you change your ways, Yahweh will bring His Temple to ruin as He did at Shiloh."

Jeremiah saw the people clench their fists and their mouths tighten, but he had more to say. "Yahweh longs to save you, but you have refused to listen to Him and have even burned your sons and daughters to false gods. You should be ashamed of yourselves. Repent now, or Yahweh will destroy you."

Tears streamed down his face and into his beard as he spoke. "The days will come when you will say, 'The harvest is past, the summer is ended, and we are not saved. Is there no balm in Gilead?' My people speak peace to their neighbors, but war springs from their hearts.

"This is what Yahweh says: 'Let not the wise man boast in his wisdom; neither let the strong man brag about his strength. If you must boast, then rejoice that you know Me, the One who created you. Repent of your evil ways, or I will toss you out and make the cities of Judah empty. I will—'"

"Let it come! Let it come!" Angry voices drowned out Jeremiah's words. "Away with this blasphemer. He must die!"

The crowd swept over Jeremiah, grabbing him, dragging him this way and that, shouting, "Kill him! Stone him! Kill him! Stone him!"

The avalanche of voices melted into a chant that reached the palace, just south of the Temple. Prince Ahikam, meeting with several other men of the royal family, glanced at them in astonishment. "What is that?"

"It sounds as if a mob wants to kill somebody," someone replied.

"We'd better check this out," Ahikam shouted over his shoulder as he bounded toward the door. "Hurry!"

21

Fire in the Gates

The royal party raced to the southeast Temple gate, just as the crowd spilled out of the court, nearly knocking them off their feet. Noticing the man at the center of the riot, the princes and nobles ran back and forth before the mob, waving their arms to stop them.

Realizing who the men were, the milling throng halted in seconds, their chanting dying while they loosened their grip on Jeremiah. The prophet's clothes hung in tatters, his nose bled, his arms, legs, chest, and back oozed with blood from countless scratches, and one eye had begun to swell.

"What goes on here?" Ahikam demanded.

"This man blasphemed the Temple, sir," Pashur said as he bowed with practiced grace. "He should be stoned."

"Without a trial?"

"No trial is necessary, sir." Pashur's anger began to filter through his forced courtesy. "Everyone heard what he said." He swept his hand toward the crowd. "There's no need for the formality of witnesses."

"Nonsense! The law condemns no man without a trial." Ahikam fought back his own growing anger. "We have several judges here." He nodded his head toward the princes behind him. "Bring your witnesses, and we shall decide this man's case."

Several men repeated the prophet's message.

"Jeremiah," Ahikam said, his eyes smiling while his expression remained serious. "You have heard these witnesses. What do you have to say for yourself?"

Bowing respectfully, Jeremiah said with a quivering voice, "They speak the truth. Yahweh commanded me to warn His people that He will punish them unless they repent." Then his voice steadied. "Treat me as you wish, sir. But you will bring the guilt of innocent blood upon this city if you kill me, for Yahweh has sent me."

The judges huddled together to decide what they should

do. The priests glared at each other, and the crowd stood so still that everyone could hear a dog barking on a nearby street.

At last Ahikam faced the people. "We find no fault in this man. He has spoken for Yahweh, so he is innocent of blasphemy."

"Amen," said an old man who stood near the front as he turned to the rest of the people. "The prophet Micah once said that Jerusalem would be destroyed," he declared.

"That's right," several of the elders agreed. They remembered their fathers telling them about it.

"Did King Hezekiah execute him?" the man continued.

"No," they agreed reluctantly.

"Then the princes are correct. We shouldn't stone Jeremiah, either."

Although the members of the mob nodded their agreement, Pashur and the other priests frowned. Ahikam saw their angry faces and turned to Jeremiah as the people drifted back into the Temple.

"Man of God," he said, "please come with us to the palace. We have a few questions."

Pashur spat on the ground in contempt as he watched the royal party leave. "We'll get him," he muttered to the other priests nearby. "We'll get him yet."

Chapter 4

Terror From the North

Dark rumors circulated throughout Judah as masses of defeated Egyptian soldiers streamed southward along the coast of the Great Sea. Jehoiakim had rebelled the year before and allied himself with Egypt. Pharaoh Necho marched his army north to Carchemish in order to protect Judah and attempt to save the remnant of the Assyrians who had holed up in that city. The Egyptian forces had faced those led by Crown Prince Nebuchadnezzar who, though only 18 years old, already commanded his father's main army.

Carchemish had importance far beyond its size, for the Euphrates River flowed so shallow at this point that soldiers could cross on foot. Control of the ford allowed easy access to either Mesopotamia, or Palestine and Egypt, depending on who held it.

Massive armies lashed each other throughout the searing day, and thousands fell dead and dying on both sides. Pharaoh's military advantage had soon disappeared, and his retreat had become a rout as Nebuchadnezzar's cavalry and battle chariots pursued him. The road to Egypt had become littered with the fallen warriors of the Nile.

Fears ran high that Babylon would conquer Egypt, and Nebuchadnezzar intended to do just that. But he felt he should first subdue Syria and Palestine. So, sending a sizable force to harry the fleeing Egyptians, he remained behind with his main army, besieging every city that refused to surrender and sending thousands of their citizens to Babylon in chains.

Jehoiakim chose to resist. "The Babylonians could never capture Jerusalem," he boasted to his courtiers. But when the enemy hordes surrounded the city like ants around a pool of honey, the king's courage failed. "They'll crush us!" he exclaimed as he imagined his own capture and execution.

While Jehoiakim wavered, Nebuchadnezzar left a large portion of his army to besiege the city and continued his march toward Egypt. In a few days he stood on its borders, prepared for the final thrust to clinch his victory over the pharaoh.

Nebuchadnezzar had been absent from Jerusalem for less than a week when a messenger arrived with Jehoiakim's surrender note. "Spare our lives," it read. "We will be your slaves."

"Good!" the Babylonian crown prince laughed. "They'll pay more taxes alive than dead. Scribe!" he called. "Prepare a reply to Jehoiakim."

"Yes, sir." The bowing scribe advanced with his papyrus brush and a broken piece of pottery that he would outline the message on.

"I accept your surrender," Nebuchadnezzar dictated. "No one will die unless you resist me when I enter your city, but I will take royal hostages with me to Babylon to guarantee your loyalty."

While the scribe finished forming the cuneiform letters by jabbing the corner of his square metal stylus on the soft surface of a new clay tablet, a royal courier from Babylon rushed in and fell at the prince's feet. "Your highness, sir," he panted, "the great king, King Nabopolassar of Babylon, has died, and your brothers are arguing over who should take the crown!"

"My brothers?" Nebuchadnezzar stormed. "They know that I have been chosen to be the next king." He turned to gaze toward Egypt, tears filling his eyes as he remembered his father. "Dead," he mumbled. But all signs of mourning vanished in an instant. "Commander!" he shouted. His chief general bowed himself into Nebuchadnezzar's presence. "I must hurry to Babylon to secure my throne. You join the siege at Jerusalem and assume command. Jehoiakim has already surrendered, and I have promised to spare his people, unless they continue to resist."

"How many hostages will you want, sir?" The general straightened.

"Oh, several thousand of the best of the city and its environs—the princes, artisans, leaders, scribes. Don't drain the city, of course, but bring me the best. Treat the hostages well, for they will be of service to me in Babylon."

"When will you leave, sir?"

"Within the hour." The prince turned, but then stopped. "I suppose we will have to forget Egypt for now. Better bring the army with you to Babylon. If my brothers give me any trouble, I may need you. If not, well, the troops could use a holiday."

"May the gods favor you, your majesty," the general said as he turned to leave.

🔥 🔥 🔥

The news of Jehoiakim's surrender swept through Jerusalem with the speed of gossip, filling every stomach with the nausea of terror. People by the thousands stampeded into Hezekiah's tunnel, climbed down into half-empty cisterns, crawled into subterranean caves below their homes—any place that appeared to offer refuge from the lustful eyes and bloodthirsty swords of the Babylonians.

The guards at East Gate opened their giant doors and ran for their lives. When the enemy entered, they found the streets deserted, save for a few stray animals.

But soon the cobblestone avenues filled with hostages, for the enemy knew all the likely places where people would hide. They injured no one, save those who resisted them, but led first one, then another, then dozens of inhabitants to the city square inside the East Gate in preparation for their journey to Babylon.

Jeremiah watched the sad affair from atop the northeast corner of the Temple walls. He knew that many of these captives were the most promising young men of the city. Some could take their wives with them, but most would travel alone. The enemy selected an occasional beautiful woman to become a concubine of the king or some nobleman and sent her off to Babylon in an ox-drawn cart.

Among the captives, Jeremiah spotted his beloved friend Daniel, the prince. Daniel's unusual intelligence, his striking good looks, and his fearless devotion to his Creator would have made him a valued advisor to the throne. What a blessing he could have been to Judah! But now, it seemed, he would languish in a Babylonian dungeon or slave away his life in some workshop.

Jeremiah wept at the injustice of the situation. "Why, Yahweh?" he demanded. "Why are You allowing them to take Daniel? Most of those hostages are pagans. But Daniel—"

He wiped his eyes with the back of his hand and glanced at an unusual movement in the Temple court below him. The sight of Babylonian soldiers striding arrogantly into the Temple precincts horrified him. A priest stepped forward to stop them, but they rudely elbowed him to one side and marched defiantly into the sacred building. Moments later they emerged, their arms loaded with sacred gold and silver bowls and other ritual objects.

Within hours Jeremiah saw the enemy with its hostages vanish toward the north. He would never again see his friends or the sacred Temple vessels.

🔥 🔥 🔥

Jeremiah descended the steps into the Temple courtyard and halted a priest who happened by. "I want to see all the chief priests and the old men in the Valley of Hinnom, outside the Dung Gate. Immediately!"

"Yes, sir." The priest frowned. He hated that meddling prophet, but obeyed his order anyway.

The priests and old men reluctantly went to the edge of the valley of Hinnom as Jeremiah had commanded. For centuries people had worshipped at pagan shrines there, but King Josiah had transformed it into a disposal sight for rubbish and dead animals.

"Why does Jeremiah want to meet us here?" Pashur grumbled. "It's hardly a place to hold an important meeting." He pinched his nose with his fingers, trying momentarily to block out the stench rising from the countless rotting carcasses strewn about the slope below him.

"I don't know what he wants," another priest complained, "but the more I hear him, the less I like him. He keeps calling the people back to the ancient laws. Imagine the chaos if they followed his advice."

"It would be disastrous to our purses," Pashur snarled.

After Jeremiah left the Temple, he stopped at a shop in the potter's quarter, chose a clay vessel, paid for it, walked to the Dung Gate on the southwest side of the city, and then out onto the ridge overlooking the Valley of Hinnom.

The priests and elders shivered as Jeremiah began talking before he even reached them. "You saw what happened today," he scolded. "The Babylonians enslaved our best people—and even plundered the sacred Temple vessels. Why?" He paused, looking into each face with a scrutiny that made all of them uneasy. But no one dared answer his question.

"I'll tell you why," he continued. "Judah has committed spiritual adultery against Yahweh by worshipping idols." An angry murmur rumbled through the group, but Jeremiah ignored it. "You claim to be Yahweh's priests, but you don't worship Him either. You worship the Temple building itself.

Instead of serving your Creator, you pay homage to His house and perform the sacred services as though they were magical ceremonies that would bring you good luck." Frustration choked his words.

"Your hearts have lost the grace of human kindness, and you think of those who were herded toward Babylon today as—as just so many bodies. Their world has come to an end, but you feel no loss. They are your sons and daughters, your brothers and sisters. But you don't care—nobody cares.

"Your ancestors burned their infants to Milcom in the Molech fire pits here in this valley. Josiah desecrated this place, but you still sacrifice your children in other fire pits. You worship the queen of heaven and all the other gods of the pagan nations around you. Will those gods spare you from the judgment of Yahweh? No! They will have no pity on you.

"You breathe easily now that the Babylonians have gone. But beware—they will return. Nebuchadnezzar is Yahweh's servant whom He has commanded to destroy this city. Today's disaster is only the beginning. Mothers will eat their children, and fathers will hate their infant sons. Thousands of people will die, and when there are no more tombs in which to bury them, their lifeless bodies will be tossed into this valley like the carcasses of the dead animals you see here today.

"Thus says Yahweh." Jeremiah raised his arm, holding the clay pot over his head. " 'I made you, like the potter formed this vessel, so you would serve Me. But you deserted Me. Therefore' "—he hurled the jar through space—" 'I will break you' "—the pot smashed against a rock, its myriad pieces tinkling over the hard ground—" 'as one breaks a potter's vessel that cannot be made whole again.' "

Chapter 5

Stocks in the Streets

"I don't like Jeremiah," one of the priests grumbled as they shuffled back through the Western Quarter from the Valley of Hinnom. "He thinks he's the only one who knows what to do."

"He claims to be a prophet," an elder replied. "We should listen to prophets."

"Prophet nothing!" Pashur sputtered. "He's a trouble-maker. I'd wager that he's in the Temple right now, inciting the people against us."

"How can you wager on a sure thing?" The first priest spit on the ground in disgust. "We've got to stop him, or he'll turn the whole city against us."

"What can we do?" the elder demanded.

"I think a riot might solve our problem," Pashur announced.

"A riot?"

"Yes," Pashur purred. "If he should create a civil disturbance, then, well, we'll have proof of his guilt, and a night in the stocks might make him consider the consequences of his actions."

The group was silent a moment, then one of the priests shouted, "Good idea, Pashur. But how can we do it?"

"Quiet down," the Temple administrator snapped as he glanced around to be sure that no one of importance could overhear them. "This is what we'll do . . ."

🔥 🔥 🔥

Jeremiah marched directly to the Temple, stepped up onto the stone bench between the two courtyards, and shouted to the assembled worshippers the same message he had given to the priests at the garbage dump. The crowds listened, spellbound—inwardly rebelling at his message, but powerless to act. Many were still dazed over the Babylonian attack. A large number of Jerusalem's inhabitants had gone into exile, never to return, and the Babylonians had looted many of the sacred Temple vessels. And now Jeremiah predicted national doom if Judah didn't repent.

"Thus says Yahweh," he thundered. His gaze seemed to penetrate the innermost souls of his listeners. "'I will bring upon you all the curses that I have spoken against you because you have stiffened your necks, and refused to obey . . .'"

"Traitor! False prophet!" a voice roared near the East Gate entrance. "Seize him!"

No one questioned the command, as they hated Jeremiah for pointing out their sins. The anonymous order crystallized their anger into mob violence, and the once silent crowd lunged toward Jeremiah.

Oh, no! he thought. *If the palace doesn't rescue me, I'm doomed!*

But instead of princes, Pashur and a small band of priests blocked his escape, and Jeremiah expected no mercy from them. Raising his hands, Pashur shouted, "Stop! Stop! Release him!"

The mob quieted and Pashur spoke again, his warm, melodious voice visibly calming it. "My dear people! Why stain your hands with blood? This man is a false prophet, so let Yahweh punish him." His smile masked his true feelings. "Don't stone him. Put him in the stocks. Give him time to meditate on his crimes."

"Good idea!" another priest shouted. "To the stocks, everyone! Let's teach Jeremiah a lesson he'll never forget."

Dragging Jeremiah with it, the mob surged toward the section near the East Gate—called the Upper Chamber of the Corner—the facilities that served as the city's temporary prison. If the distance had been but a few more cubits, the frenzied people would have wrenched his arms from their sockets.

But the stocks gave Jeremiah no relief. They confined him in an uncomfortable position that made it impossible for him to relax his strained muscles. An overnight stay could reduce some men to hysteria, while those left several days often required medical treatment.

The mob taunted Jeremiah for more than an hour, but one by one, the people tired of their sport. Before long the prophet languished alone.

🔥 🔥 🔥

Jeremiah had been in the stocks for about two hours, and his body had begun to throb with pain. Though no one stood nearby, it seemed that a voice whispered into his ear: "Write down the messages you've been preaching."

How can I write when I'm locked in these stocks? he thought. As he wrestled with his feelings he watched the people who passed the chamber. A familiar face drifted into view—a scribe with a scroll tucked under his arm.

"Baruch! Baruch!" Jeremiah yelled. The man stopped, fingered his scroll, and glanced around. "Over here, Baruch."

As Baruch hurried toward his friend, he gasped. "Jeremiah! What are you doing in the stocks?"

"I preached Yahweh's message in the Temple, and the people didn't like it." The prophet sighed. "Where are you going?"

"To seek work at the palace." He held up his scroll and

writing satchel. "My brother Seraiah told me that the king might appoint me to an important position. It's a good opportunity, don't you think? I could become a high official."

"What's written on that scroll, Baruch?" The prophet ignored his friend's enthusiasm.

"Nothing yet." He took the scroll from under his arm, untied the leather thongs, and unrolled a few inches so Jeremiah could see it. "I made it myself."

Wincing with pain, the prophet studied the handiwork of his friend. "It's a fine scroll, Baruch."

The scribe rolled up his scroll again and looked at Jeremiah. "Is there anything I can do for you?"

"Yes," the prophet spoke slowly, choosing his words carefully. "Yahweh wants me to write down the messages He has given me. But I need someone to do it. Baruch, could you locate a scribe who would sit beside these stocks and write what I tell him?"

The color drained from Baruch's face. He saw a man suffering in the stocks and heard his strained voice, but his own cherished dreams raced through his head. The goal of every person who could read and write was advancement through service in the palace. As a scribe to the king, perhaps one day Baruch could even become prime minister. The throbbing of the pulse in his throat threatened to choke him. *What will happen to all my plans,* he wondered, *if I act as a scribe for a hated prophet? It will likely bring shame, persecution, and an early grave.*

Baruch struggled with Jeremiah's request for some minutes. Finally, he told the prophet in a choked voice, "I will write your messages." He sat down on the edge of the raised platform, and with quaking hands unrolled a portion of his new scroll. Taking a reed pen from the writing case that hung at his side, he began mixing some water with the dried ink on his scribal palette before looking at Jeremiah. "What would you like me to write?"

Fire in the Gates

All afternoon the prophet dictated with a tired voice, and Baruch brushed the letters onto the surface of the new parchment. Line by line the scroll filled with Yahweh's messages as preached by Jeremiah the prophet.

Finally the two men finished their work. Baruch was exhausted, his fingers cramped from long hours of forming Hebrew letters.

Jeremiah's face was pale, and he seemed near fainting. He was certain he would die if someone didn't release him, but he couldn't think of that now.

"Baruch." His hoarse voice began to fade. "Thank you. Find someone—read the scroll—at the morning sacrifice."

The scribe's stomach tightened into a knot. Reading such messages in the Temple would surely cause another riot. And whoever did could expect no better treatment than Jeremiah had received. Baruch felt a strange chill pass over him, but he ignored it. "I—I'll read it at this morning's service, sir."

"May Yahweh bless you, Baru . . ." Jeremiah closed his eyes.

The scribe packed his writing equipment into the carrying case. He slid its strap over his head, retrieved the scroll, and turned his weary feet toward the Temple.

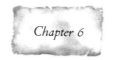

Chapter 6

Blazing Parchment

"Baruch! Wait!"

The scribe spun on his heels to see who had called his name. In the dimness of the predawn hour, he saw Jeremiah hobbling up the street toward him.

"How did you get out of prison?" He had so dreaded reading Jeremiah's scroll in the Temple that the prophet's unexpected appearance now unnerved him.

"I had a word from Yahweh, Baruch." Jeremiah put a hand on his friend's shoulder. "He asked me to delay reading the scroll until a national feast, and when I awoke this morning, the jailer released me." The prophet noticed the tension leave Baruch's body as the scribe realized that he wouldn't have to read the scroll that morning.

"Where are you lodging, Baruch?"

"I have no place yet." He did not mention the uncomfortable night he had spent in a dark corner on a side street.

"Why not stay with me?"

"I would be honored."

The prophet squeezed his companion's arm as the two strolled off toward Jeremiah's home. "It's good to have one true friend in this wicked city."

🔥 🔥 🔥

Several months passed, and royal messengers announced that the Babylonian army had laid siege to Ashkelon, 45 miles to the west, on the coast of the Great Sea. No one doubted that Jerusalem would be next.

King Jehoiakim knew that Jerusalem could never survive a full-scale siege, and so he had not prepared for one. The food storehouses stood empty; Hezekiah's tunnel water system needed cleaning and repair; the weapons arsenals bulged with rusting or corroded weapons that could never withstand a major battle; and the troops were ill-trained and demoralized.

The king had spent the past three years building a new cedar palace, painting it in the style of the great houses of Egypt. It told the world that his ties lay with the pharaoh.

The inhabitants of Jerusalem hated the king's palace! Jehoiakim had hired local craftsmen, magnanimously supplied their food and lodging while they worked, but then refused to pay their wages when they finished their assignments. Other workers, who had not yet finished their tasks, laid down their tools when they discovered his scheme. So Jehoiakim enslaved them all, forcing them to finish the project without even the promise of payment. His brazen act enraged the entire country.

But now Nebuchadnezzar approached, and Jehoiakim panicked. He knew that he must regain the support of his alienated people in order to save his throne, and he cast about for some workable plan.

"Perhaps you could win their allegiance by appointing a day of fasting and prayer," one of his counselors suggested.

Although he disliked the concept, the king accepted the idea. "The people will pray to Yahweh, and Yahweh will save them." He smiled at the thought of ignorant people meekly following his suggestions. "That ought to get their minds off my new palace."

🔥 🔥 🔥

At the time for the morning sacrifice on Jehoiakim's "National Day of Fasting and Prayer," Baruch strolled into the Temple with Jeremiah's scroll tucked under his arm. No one paid him any attention when he stepped up onto the stone bench between the courts and turned toward the people, but every eye darted his way when he unrolled a portion of the scroll. No one recognized him or knew what he would say, but the opening sentence announced that the contents came from Jeremiah.

Baruch read in the monotone he had learned in scribal school, but everyone heard the message. Some hearts softened, others hardened, and still others seethed with anger. But no one blamed Baruch. They merely hated Jeremiah all the more for hiring a scribe to deliver his hostile message.

When Baruch finished reading, he rerolled the scroll and elbowed his way through the crowd, while the people turned their attention back to the Temple service. Their indifference puzzled the scribe. He'd expected them to throw him out, or even to stone him. But he never dreamed they would just ignore him.

The scribe had almost cleared the southeast Temple gate when a strong hand gripped his shoulder, sending a jolt of fear through his body. *This is it!* he thought. *I will pay for my act—perhaps with my life!* But when he turned around he gazed into the eyes of a smiling man who wore a red cloth belt.

"You have great courage to read that scroll here," the royal stranger said.

"I've only done my duty."

"You have done it well. But the man who should have heard it was not here today."

"The king?"

"Yes, and the other princes as well." The man placed both thumbs into his red sash. "I'm the only member of the royal family who attended the Temple service this morning. Surprising, too, since my father ordered the fast."

"That does seem strange," Baruch agreed.

"But if Jeremiah is right, he won't get away with it." The prince frowned as he gazed back toward the worshipping people. After a moment's silence he smiled. "Baruch, if I can arrange it, would you read this scroll to the rest of the court?"

"Of course." The scribe's desire to serve in the palace returned, creating a simultaneous sense of excitement and fear.

"Good," the prince said as he stroked his beard. "I'll meet you here after the evening sacrifice. Bring the scroll with you."

"Very well." Baruch hurried home.

"I'm glad you're safe." Jeremiah's voice revealed his concern.

"So am I," the scribe admitted, "but there was no need to worry. The people ignored me. When I finished reading, they turned back to watch the ritual as though nothing had happened."

"That was good for you, Baruch, but it's bad for them." Sitting on a stool, Jeremiah put his face in his hands. "Those people have become so calloused that they no longer hear the voice of Yahweh."

"One person heard."

"Oh?" The prophet looked up, surprised. "Who?"

Baruch related his encounter with the prince. "I don't know his name, but I plan to see him this evening."

"Sounds like Michaiah to me. He's a good man. If he wants the king to hear this message, it's worth our time to do it. He won't lead us into a trap."

After the evening Temple service, Baruch stood beside the gate, curious to discover what the prince had arranged. When Michaiah arrived, the scribe immediately asked, "Did you have any success?"

"Yes. The princes have agreed to listen to the scroll, but they warned me that you and Jeremiah will be in danger when the king hears it."

"Thanks for your concern," Baruch sighed, "but that's our problem."

"We'll help you," Michaiah assured him. "Come with me."

The two walked out of the southeastern Temple gate and turned west toward the palace. But instead of entering the royal palace, they opened a door that led into a chamber within the Temple wall. Baruch's eyes strained as he peered into the dim enclosure, lighted only by olive oil lamps set into small niches in the walls. Soft shadows obscured the red-sashed men who sat on the long benches placed around the perimeter of the room, and Baruch didn't recognize any of them.

Michaiah barred the door before turning to the others.

"My friends, this is Baruch, and he will read the scroll of the prophet Jeremiah."

The men shifted restlessly in their seats as the scribe unrolled a portion of the scroll and held it near one of the lamps. As he read it he glanced up from time to time to see how the message affected his listeners. Some faces scowled with hostility and others radiated humility and kindness.

When he had finished reading, Baruch rerolled the scroll, as Michaiah stood. "Should the king hear this message?"

"Yes," grunted several princes in unison.

"By all means," one man added as he stood and crossed his arms, "but it will make him angry. He will kill Jeremiah and Baruch." He paused, then seemed to choose his words carefully. "Remember the prophet Urijah?" A chorus of groans filled the room, and the person sitting next to the speaker buried his face in his hands. The one who had spoken gently patted the shoulder of the grieving man as he continued. "The king had Elnathan, here, chase Urijah all the way to Egypt and bring him back. Then his highness killed the prophet with his royal sword. We must take care, my friends, for I believe Jeremiah and this scribe could meet the same fate if we read that scroll to the king."

"You're right," Michaiah agreed, "so we must hide Jeremiah and Baruch before Jehoiackim hears the scroll."

"Well spoken," Gemariah, the man to whom the chamber belonged, commented. "Hide them first. The king acts quickly when he's angry."

Jeremiah and Baruch moved into the home of a casual friend after dark that evening and trusted Yahweh to protect them from the wrath of the king.

🔥 🔥 🔥

The princes entered the palace together, taking with them the palace scribe Jehudi, who carried the scroll.

"Well, well," Jehoiakim said from his padded chair as the men entered his chamber. "What brings you here this evening?" Noticing their expressions, he commented, "You look as if you've been to a funeral." Then with a laugh he rose to warm himself before a small brazier.

"We may soon attend our own," Delaiah said, "unless we follow the instructions of Yahweh."

"What makes you think we haven't?" the king sneered.

"Because Yahweh Himself has said so, sir." He pointed to the scroll.

The king bristled. "What scroll is that? Who wrote it?"

"The prophet Jeremiah," Gemariah answered. "Baruch, the scribe, read it at the Temple this morning. We thought you should hear it too."

"All right," the king sighed as he sank back onto his chair, "let's get it over with."

Unrolling the scroll, Jehudi began to read. A range of emotions flickered across Jehoiakim's face—perplexity evolved into shock and fear, quickly exploding into anger. After a few moments he lunged toward Jehudi, grabbed the scroll, and rushed back to the brazier.

Gemariah, Delaiah, and Elnathan surged forward

together, attempting to stop the king from destroying the scroll, but they were already too late. The king slashed it with a knife and tossed the pieces into the fire. Acrid smoke filled the room as the leather burned.

"Your majesty!" Gemariah protested. "You shouldn't have done that!"

"Why not?" Jehoiakim shouted. "I am king, am I not? And I'll do the same to the men who wrote it. Guard!" he roared. "Fetch me Jeremiah and Baruch. Quickly! I'm going to kill them both!"

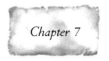

Chapter 7

Here We Go Again

"Yahweh has a message for Jehoiakim," Jeremiah told Baruch the day after the king burned the scroll. He knelt in the courtyard behind his friend's room, beside an open fire in a round pit built of broken pieces of pottery cemented together with clay. He raked the coals onto two stone slabs and added several sticks so the fire would reach the proper temperature. When the stones became hot enough, he would sweep off the ashes and cook bread dough on them—flat cakes of wheat or barley flour mixed with oil and water. After stirring a pot of lentil porridge at the rear of the pit, he turned again to Baruch.

The scribe sat cross-legged with a papyrus scroll unrolled before him and brushed the point of his pen in the ink "What does God wish to tell his majesty?"

"Write this: 'Woe to him who builds by wrongdoing and refuses to pay his workers. Do you rule Judah because you live in a cedar palace? No. Yahweh requires that you execute righteousness and justice, but your heart swells with greed, and you have killed innocent people.'

"Therefore, thus says Yahweh: 'Your people will not weep when you die. As a slave disposes of a dead donkey, so they will drag you beyond the gates of Jerusalem and throw you onto the garbage dump. For I, Yahweh, have spoken it.'"

Baruch seemed quieter than usual. "He will search everywhere for us."

"Yes, but he'll never find us." Jeremiah smiled. "Come,

Baruch, we have work to do. Yahweh wants us to rewrite the scroll that Jehoiakim burned."

"Write it again?" Baruch recalled the new scroll he had made and his shock when he learned how Jehoiakim destroyed it. *And to think,* he mused, *I wanted to serve him! How fortunate that Jeremiah rescued me from slavery to so ruthless a king! I may never become a great man in Judah, but I will fill my days with joyful service to my God.*

"All right," Baruch reined in his thoughts. "Here we go again."

Instead of writing the entire scroll in one sitting as they had done before, the two men spent parts of several days working on the project. Jeremiah also added several things that God had given him since the original message so that the new document contained more than the one Jehoiakim had burned.

"No one can destroy Yahweh's word despite what the king may think." Jeremiah smiled as they completed the scroll. "God will cause people to hear His word in spite of their efforts to silence His prophets."

♦ ♦ ♦

Jehoiakim's guards pounded on countless doors as they searched for the pair before they gave up in despair. "Jeremiah and Baruch must have fled the city," they reported to the king. "We've turned Jerusalem upside down, but we find no trace of them."

"I know they're here!" the monarch thundered. "Look what they sent me this morning." Unrolling the prophecy of his doom, he tossed it into the face of the royal officer.

"Where did you get this?" the captain asked as he examined the scroll.

"The steward got it from a servant, who took it from a merchant, who said that someone left it in his shop." The king paced before his throne.

"They covered their tracks well."

The king ignored him. "If I could get hold of that prophet and his scribe, I'd kill them with my own hands."

"I'm sure you would," one of the guards mumbled to himself.

"What did you say?" Jehoiakim screamed.

"I—I—I said," the guard stuttered, blanching with fear, "I wish we could find them."

"So do I!" the king's face reddened. "Now get back out there and get them!"

"Yes, sir!"

The soldiers had never been so happy to leave the king's presence. While he had always been unpleasant to deal with, now every servant feared a summons to his chambers, for no one knew what the ruler would do next.

A messenger entered as the guards departed. "Your Majesty," he announced, "Egypt and Babylon are at war again."

"Wonderful." The king smiled, rubbing his hands together. "If Egypt wins, we'll have our freedom back."

🔥 🔥 🔥

The battle zigzagged through the day, and Nebuchadnezzar cursed his gods that the bulk of his army fought elsewhere. He couldn't retrieve them for this battle, and without them he knew he couldn't win. While his generals, weapons, and soldiers outclassed those of Egypt, he didn't have enough men. By evening he ordered a retreat to prevent total disaster.

During the days following, Pharaoh tried in vain to pin his enemy down and destroy him, but Nebuchadnezzar eluded him. Crossing the ford at Carchemish, the Babylonian king won and lost at the same time—he escaped annihilation at the hands of Egypt, but he had to relinquish control of Palestine.

Jehoiakim rejoiced when he learned that the Egyptians had driven Nebuchadnezzar from the area. "Go home," he ordered the Babylonian ambassador, "and if you don't leave today, I'll turn you over to Egypt as a spy, and you know what they do to spies."

"I'll go," the envoy replied as he bowed politely. "But sir, when Nebuchadnezzar returns, he will punish you if you stop paying—"

"He's not coming back!" Jehoiakim shouted. "Egypt will see to that."

"As you say." The envoy bowed again. "But Your Majesty is making a terrible mistake."

"Guards!" the king screamed. "Throw this man out!"

The Egyptian ambassador waited outside the throne room as the guards escorted the Babylonian out of the palace. "Pleasant journey, friend." He smiled at the official. "Watch out for our scouts—they might think you're a spy." Then laughing at his little joke, he entered the royal chamber.

"Ah, Your Majesty, I see you have smoothed the road for the lord of the Nile."

"Yes." Jehoiakim seemed pleased with himself. "We have abandoned Babylon, and now we desire to once again ally with Egypt. Will Pharaoh accept us?"

The ambassador's smile showed his delight. "Your return will make him happy, for he fought this war with Babylon because of you."

"He will not be half as happy over our return as I am," Jehoiakim said, remembering that Egypt's taxes were less than those of Nebuchadnezzar. "Babylon may seek to return," he said cautiously, "but we will depend on you for help."

"We will do all we can."

Chapter 8

A Donkey's Funeral

"Curse those Babylonians!" Jehoiakim shouted at his council.

"But the desert raiders aren't Babylonians," his prime minister reminded him.

"I know, I know! But Nebuchadnezzar supports them." Jehoiakim hated those who advised him. *If I could only find capable men whom I could trust,* he thought, *I'd replace every one of these fools.* But, even though he did not yet realize it, he had executed or exiled all the trustworthy individuals in Judah.

"We've tried to stop the raiders," the general protested with a shrug. "As soon as we receive a plea for help, we march to the rescue, but when we arrive, the raiders have gone, and—"

"And they've taken scores of captives with them," the prime minister interrupted, pacing before the throne. Although his official title was "cupbearer," for he tasted the king's wine, checking it for poison, his position of trust also made him the prime minister. He acted as intercessor between the people and their king. "We've lost several thousand people already."

"To say nothing of gold, silver, livestock, and food." The king chafed more at the material losses than the human misery.

"Why don't we ask Egypt for help?" the general suggested. "They promised us military aid."

"We could." The king put a forefinger to his lips and

stared out the window, deep in thought. "But there couldn't be more than a few hundred raiders, and we should be able to handle them ourselves. If we called on Egypt, all the world would know how helpless we've become."

"I see." The military leader remained silent for some time. "Then let's put more men into the towns so we can catch the raiders before they strike."

"Fine," the king agreed, pointing accusingly at the general, "but keep a strong force in Jerusalem. We don't want to be caught out in the country if Nebuchadnezzar returns."

"We'll be careful," the general sighed as he left the room.

The raiders continued their attacks, destroying more towns, killing and capturing more people and livestock, and carrying everything of value into the desert. Judah's army had pursued the raiders many times, but after several years, they could only count an occasional enemy destroyed, and they hadn't prevented a single excursion.

The people of Judah suffered terribly, and unrest blossomed on every side. "If our soldiers can't stop small bands of thieves," they protested, "how can they protect us from a large scale invasion?"

🔥 🔥 🔥

Nebuchadnezzar returned to Palestine after an absence of eight years and once again surrounded Jerusalem. Jehoiakim had known of the enemy's approach, but told only a few top officials when they secretly met to decide what to do. Should they resist or surrender?

"Surrender?" the general fussed. "Not without a fight. Otherwise the nations will think we have no strength at all."

"But if we hold out too long the Babylonians will become angry," the prime minister cautioned. "Then when we do surrender, they will execute many of us."

Fire in the Gates

"I don't see how fighting will help at all," Jehoiakim fumed, his anger growing with his frustration. "Our armies have floundered before those desert thieves for eight years. What sense will it make to resist now?"

"You know how swiftly those desert rats move," the general barked, jumping to his feet.

"I know! I know!" Jehoiakim shouted at him. "And I've also seen the speed of your military snails! I have never seen such incompetence in my life!" He gritted his teeth as he spat out the words. "And you want to fight Nebuchadnezzar. If he doesn't skin you alive, I will!"

Shocked silence filled the council chamber for several minutes as Jehoiakim glared at his advisors. No one dared so much as to clear his throat. When the king spoke again, his voice sounded quieter than before. "Surrender seems our only hope. Nebuchadnezzar treated us kindly before, and perhaps he'll favor us again."

"Idiocy!" the general exploded.

"Silence, you shield pounder!" the king warned as he jumped to his feet and whipped out his sword. "Get out of my sight!"

The furious soldier stalked from the room, mumbling to himself, "We'll see if he surrenders. I'm still general—I command the troops!"

The other counselors, distraught by the king's violent tantrum, withdrew from the room, and Jehoiakim summoned a scribe to dictate his surrender message to Nebuchadnezzar. "We have no desire to fight. We will open our gates, as we did before, and permit your armies to enter. Please treat us kindly."

After dispatching a royal courier who would pass the message over the wall to the Babylonians, he returned to his throne, anger and uncertainty gnawing at his stomach. *Surrendering to a major army causes me no embarrassment,* he thought, *for victory is impossible. But for my leading general to fly in my face—unthinkable!*

"I must replace that man," he announced to his prime minister, who had returned to the room. "Well, not just now—perhaps after the Babylonians leave."

The messenger returned with Nebuchadnezzar's answer within the hour. "I will accept your surrender. Meet my delegates in the square at the East Gate to arrange for hostages."

Nebuchadnezzar's own seal graced the clay message tablet.

Soon Jehoiakim's entourage paraded toward the East Gate, flanked by his personal guard. The city streets lay empty, and the walls ahead of him bristled with armed men. The king's gaze, fixed on the gate, failed to notice that his archers had strung their bows with arrows.

When he reached the city square, he ordered the gatekeepers to open the great cedar doors, and the procession paused as the huge gates swung inward on their massive stone sockets. The king eyed the fierce multitude waiting outside behind the official occupation party. His heart skipped a beat when he recognized the chief Babylonian officer as the ambassador whom he had insulted eight years before.

The Babylonian delegation began to advance, while Jehoiakim's group waited about 75 feet inside the gate. As the envoys neared, Jehoiakim began to kneel, as custom demanded.

Suddenly arrows showered from the archers on the wall! Ambush!

Jehoiakim panicked as the battle exploded all around him and he stood unarmed. Terrified, the king fled, his soldiers parting to allow him passage, then closing ranks to face the enemy. It was no use. The gate stood open, and Babylonians rushed into the city by the thousands, killing people everywhere.

A band of Babylonian commandos chased the fleeing

Jewish king as he raced through the Western Quarter seeking some sanctuary. They fought off his bodyguard and cornered him in a dead-end street.

Cruel hands grabbed the king, shackled him in iron, and jerked him roughly about. He gasped for mercy as they began to drag him back toward the East Gate, but their angry shouts drowned out his pleas.

The Babylonians had not gone far before they realized that their royal prisoner no longer resisted. Jehoiakim was dead.

Without delay, four of the men lifted the lifeless body and marched under armed escort through the Dung Gate into the Valley of Hinnom and to the brink of the city dump. Below them lay the rotting carcasses and bleached skeletons of countless dead animals—thrown over the edge to be devoured by birds of prey and wild dogs. The Babylonians tossed the still-shackled royal corpse onto the pile of putrefying bodies, turned about-face, and returned to the city.

🔥 🔥 🔥

Nebuchadnezzar placed 18-year-old Jehoiachin, the oldest son of Jehoiakim, on the throne of Judah for three months while the Babylonian army continued its Palestinian campaign. But Nebuchadnezzar didn't trust him. So he took him to Babylon along with his mother, his wives, his concubines, and his children. Then he set Mattaniah, a brother of Jehoiakim, on the throne and changed his name to Zedekiah.

Chapter 9

The Linen Belt

"What a beautiful belt," Baruch exclaimed as he eyed the linen sash around Jeremiah's waist.

"I'm happy you like it," the prophet, now in his mid-40s, replied. He and Baruch were glad to be back in their own home. They had spent several years hiding from the vengeful wrath of Jehoiakim.

"But wasn't it expensive?" Baruch whistled through his teeth. "How can you afford such luxury?" The scribe put his forefinger under the edge of the belt and savored its smooth, stiff texture.

"Yahweh asked me to buy it and take it with me on a journey." Jeremiah ran his hands through his salt-and-pepper hair as he removed his knapsack from a hook on the wall.

"Where are you going?"

"To the Euphrates River." He removed his new linen belt, folded it, and placed it in the knapsack.

"Why are you going?"

Scratching his head, the prophet replied, "I don't know just yet. I suppose it must be an object lesson to help me explain God's plan to the people."

"May I go with you?"

"Of course, if you like. But the trip will be long and dangerous."

"Then I must go," the scribe said, reaching for his own knapsack. "It's not good for a single person to go so far alone. When do we leave?"

"As soon as we can. Would you mind rolling up our sleeping mats?"

Jeremiah carefully packed the food and other needed items. He included wine, oil, and some clean rags in case of injuries. Closing their bags, Jeremiah and Baruch pulled the straps over their heads so that the knapsacks hung from their right shoulders and rested against the left hips. Then, taking their walking sticks, the two men started for the city gate.

First they stopped at the Temple treasury so that Jeremiah could draw his monthly priest's pay in small bars of silver instead of the usual food rations. The Temple steward recognized him, but treated him as gruffly as he had on the first night the prophet met him.

Passing through the East Gate, Jeremiah and Baruch strolled down the hill and across the trickle of water called the Kidron. Skirting the northwestern flank of the Mount of Olives, they headed toward Anathoth, bypassing the town because of the continued hostility of Jeremiah's uncles. Just south of the city of Dan they caught a caravan following the trade route through the desert to Damascus. From Damascus, after a two-day rest, the caravan traveled up the Abana River Valley to Helbon and then turned northeast up the Subat Valley to Zedad. From there it went northward to Hamath, and on to Tiphsah on the Euphrates River.

They had journeyed 350 miles in about three weeks. After a good night's sleep, Jeremiah and Baruch headed east along the river bank until they found a large group of rocks near the water's edge. Seeming to recognize the spot, Jeremiah searched until he found a rock with a strange-shaped hole in it. He took his knapsack from his shoulder, unpacked the new linen belt, and stuffed it into the hole, placing a stone in front of it to hide the opening.

Both men then returned to Jerusalem over the same

torturous terrain and rested from their travels. Weeks passed, ones filled with incessant activity. Jeremiah and Baruch talked daily with people in the streets and studied the teaching of Scripture with them in their homes. They emphasized God's love for His people and the judgments Judah faced if it continued to worship false gods.

"Nebuchadnezzar will return," they insisted. "Do not resist him, or you will die. Your only safety lies in total surrender to the conquerors." The strange message smacked of treason, even to Jeremiah and Baruch.

Then one day the order came: return to the Euphrates River, find the linen belt, and bring it back to Jerusalem.

Once more the pair made the grueling 350-mile journey to the distant river, traversing the mountains, deserts, and valleys of foreign lands until they stood once more on the banks of the great eastern river.

Finding the hole in the rock where he had hidden the belt, Jeremiah removed the stone from its opening. The belt had become moldy and insect-eaten. He folded it carefully into another cloth, so as not to soil his clothes, packed it in his knapsack, and returned to Jerusalem.

🔥 🔥 🔥

Back in the holy city once more, Jeremiah entered the Temple at the time of the morning sacrifice, stepped up onto the stone bench between the courtyards, and held up the moldy belt. "Many of you know that I have traveled to the Euphrates River twice in recent months, but you don't know why.

"On my first trip, Yahweh had me place this belt in the hole of a rock, and on my second journey I retrieved it. The belt was new when I buried it, but look at it now—full of holes.

"Thus says Yahweh: 'As a belt fastens to a man's waist, so I have caused you to cling to Me. You should have been a special people, bringing glory to My name, but you would not listen to Me. For that reason I will mar the pride of Judah and Jerusalem. Since you refuse to hear my words and have worshipped strange gods instead of serving Me, you will become like this worm-eaten belt—good for nothing.'"

Chapter 10

Duel in the Temple

"Hear the word of the Lord."

Jeremiah looked up from the place where he prayed to see who had spoken. A priest stood on the stone bench between the courts where Jeremiah himself had often delivered his messages from Yahweh.

"Be of good cheer," the smiling priest declared. "Yahweh will rescue the captives and break Nebuchadnezzar's neck. Jehoiachin and all his servants will return and will bring the holy vessels back to Yahweh's Temple. Do not fear, for it will come to pass within two years."

As he listened Jeremiah fingered the wooden neck yoke that God had instructed him to wear. It dramatized Yahweh's predictions that Judah must submit to Babylon for 70 years, but now this man claimed the captives would return in two years. His message would encourage the people to resist Babylon rather than to submit to its rule.

Striding toward the speaker, Jeremiah pointed his finger at the man. "Whom do you think you are to lie like that?"

"I am Hananiah, the prophet of Yahweh." The man raised his chin and glared at Jeremiah. "I have been shown, sir!"—he spat the word out along with a shower of saliva—"that you are a false prophet, sent by the evil one to discourage the people." Hananiah stepped down from his perch, strutted over to Jeremiah, and broke the wooden yoke off the prophet's neck.

"Thus says Yahweh," he shouted. "As I have plucked

this yoke from Jeremiah's neck, so God will remove Babylon's yoke from Judah's neck. Within two years," he thundered, "we shall have peace, and Babylon will plague us no more."

"Therefore," Hananiah continued, "tell the nations around us that we will unite with them to fight against Babylon, and God will give us victory!"

The crowd roared their approval of the handsome prophet's message. Those presented by Jeremiah always depressed them, but this man's oracles always cheered them.

Jeremiah cornered him before he could leave. "Hananiah, I wish Babylon would fall so our people, our king, and our holy vessels could be returned to us. But it will not be." Raising his voice, Jeremiah declared, "Thus says Yahweh: 'You have broken a wooden yoke, but I will shackle Judah in iron, and she shall serve Babylon 70 years.'" The words fell like hammer blows.

Then he turned toward the crowd. "You may remember my prediction that Jehoiakim would die and rot like a dead donkey in the Valley of Hinnom." He paused to let them recall the incident. "He died just as I described. And Nebuchadnezzar deported his son, too, exactly as I said he would. If God has fulfilled my predictions in the past, then He has also revealed that Babylon will rule us for 70—"

"Lies!" Hananiah screamed, his eyes flashing. "Yahweh hasn't sent you at all. I—I am the true prophet, and I predict peace in two years."

"Very well, Hananiah." Jeremiah's jaw tightened. "You prophesy of peace, and I predict captivity. The prophet who predicts peace, when that prophet's word shall come to pass, then we will know that Yahweh has truly sent him."

"I'll accept that," Hananiah stormed. "When peace comes, everyone will know that Yahweh has sent me. Then,

Jeremiah, then you will be disgraced." Hananiah's voice rose to a high pitch. "We ought to stone you!" he screeched, clenching his fists. "A prophet of Yahweh? Ha!"

Then he forced himself into an icy calm. "We'll grant you mercy until Jehoiachin returns from Babylon. But then, Jeremiah, then we'll stone you for your false prophecies."

"You will wait a long time," Jeremiah chuckled. "Jehoiachin will die in Babylon."

"You infidel! How dare you contradict a prophet of God?"

Jeremiah just stared at him before turning and walking away. Sometime later he waited for Hananiah to appear in the Temple precincts. Planting himself in front of the priest, he said, "Thus says Yahweh: 'Behold, Hananiah, I will cast you to the face of the earth. This very year you will die because you have fostered rebellion among My people.'"

The unmistakable authority in Jeremiah's voice caused Hananiah to draw back in terror. For several seconds the man stood there, unable to move. Then he fled through the crowds toward the Temple gate.

As Jeremiah watched him leave, he noticed Zedekiah standing near the gate that led into East Street. "The prophet who predicts peace," Jeremiah repeated loud enough for the king to hear, "when that prophet's word shall come to pass, then you will know that Yahweh has truly sent him."

Hananiah made several appearances in the Temple and elsewhere around the city, speaking of the impending peace he believed would come in two years, but his authority had evaporated like water on a hot stone. Fear haunted his eyes, and few paid him any attention.

🔥 🔥 🔥

One morning, several months after Jeremiah's verbal duel with Hananiah in the Temple, a funeral procession crawled down East Street toward the burial grounds on the Mount of Olives. Hired mourners, dressed in sackcloth and covered with ash, wailed around the covered bier. But one woman walking in front of the litter caught Jeremiah's eye, for her grief was genuine. She was Hananiah's wife.

The false prophet was dead.

Chapter 11

Yokes for the Necks of Kings

When Jeremiah reached home after encountering Hananiah's funeral procession, he found Baruch weeping. "What's the trouble, my friend?" He laid his hand on the scribe's shoulder.

"The captives have revolted in Babylon," he sobbed.

"That's terrible," Jeremiah groaned. "Nebuchadnezzar will crush them, and hundreds will die." He paced the floor in circles, deep in thought. "No doubt news of Hananiah's preaching gave them false hopes. Who told you?"

"My brother Seraiah who works in the palace. He also said that King Zedekiah has been summoned to Babylon to pledge his loyalty." Baruch wiped his eyes with the back of his hand.

"It's that serious?"

"Yes, Jeremiah. Nebuchadnezzar thinks Zedekiah is behind it."

"He's not, but some of his advisors might have something to do with it. When is he going?"

"Tomorrow. I think my brother will accompany the royal delegation."

"Then that explains the vision I received last night." Jeremiah sat down on a stool near his friend and stared through the square opening in the wall up at the sky. "The message is for the exiled people of Judah." He motioned toward the scribe's writing case sitting on a shelf. "Baruch, get a piece of pottery and compose a letter for me."

Baruch jotted down the message that Jeremiah dictated. "To the exiles who live in Babylon: Build homes, raise families, establish businesses, plant vineyards, settle yourselves in Babylon, for most of you will spend the rest of your lives there. Don't listen to anyone who tells you that the captivity will end soon, for believing such lies will only bring trouble upon you."

Jeremiah gave more counsel, instructed Baruch on how it should be read to the people and suggested that Elasah son of Shaphan and Gemariah son of Hilkiah whom Zedekiah planned to send to King Nebuchadnezzar in Babylon should present it to the exiles.

🔥 🔥 🔥

When Zedekiah appeared before Nebuchadnezzar in Babylon, the pagan king demanded that he swear his allegiance in the name of Yahweh. Nebuchadnezzar knew Daniel's unerring loyalty to Yahweh, and thought, *Surely Zedekiah will also respect an oath sworn in the name of his God.*

Meanwhile, visiting the Judahite exiles, Elasah and Gemariah gathered several leaders and a crowd of people on the west bank of the Euphrates River and read Jeremiah's scroll despite the objections of Ahab son of Kolaiah and Zedekiah son of Maaseiah, two self-appointed prophets who lived there. Then, following Jeremiah's instructions, they tied the scroll to a large rock and threw it into the river and rejoined King Zedekiah at the Babylonian palace.

🔥 🔥 🔥

Ahab and Zedekiah, the false prophets, publicly opposed Jeremiah's message, rallying many exiles to their cause in open revolt. But the Babylonian forces squashed the riot, killing hundreds in the process. They captured the two false prophets and brought them before Nebuchadnezzar, who personally judged them. Through his spies the king had learned of their sedition and of Jeremiah's efforts to stop it. Since the two men had created the rebellion, Nebuchadnezzar condemned them to death for their treason.

The Babylonian king directed that Ahab and Zedekiah be executed on the same river bank from which they had listened to Jeremiah's letter. Royal engineers constructed a fire pit with two stout poles stretched across it. Then soldiers strapped Ahab and Zedekiah to the poles and rotated them slowly over the flames until they died—roasted alive.

🔥 🔥 🔥

King Zedekiah and his entourage returned to Jerusalem to find ambassadors from several surrounding nations gathered at the palace.

"We despise Babylon's tyranny," the envoy from Edom declared, bowing from the waist as he spoke. "We prefer that Egypt coordinate our affairs."

"Yes," joined in the Ammonite ambassador. "Pharaoh taxes us, but he never drags our people to Egypt."

"Sometimes he does it to punish a nation for withholding taxes," the Moabite representative reminded them.

"True," the Ammonite grunted, frowning, "but not from general policy. If we would all unite with Egypt, I believe Babylon would leave us alone."

"That's right," agreed the ambassador from Tyre. "Egypt has mauled Babylon several times, and if we had supported it, might even have destroyed Babylon altogether by now."

"You embarrass me." Zedekiah held up his hands in an effort to stop them. "I've just returned from Babylon, and while there I took an oath to remain loyal to Nebuchadnezzar."

"But you needn't fear to break your word," the Sidonian delegate laughed. "We will protect each other."

"I wish I could believe that." Zedekiah scowled. "But it does sound good." The Judahite king could never make up his mind for himself and often allowed advisors to draft his policies. Friends and enemies alike pushed him this way and that, while despising him and fearing to trust his word.

"Our alliance will work." The Edomite smiled. "Pharaoh will welcome and protect us—with his full army, if need be. We have nothing to fear."

At that precise moment Jeremiah entered the room and began distributing strange wooden objects to the ambassadors. At first the men took them as gifts from Zedekiah, but one look at his expression banished that idea.

"These are yokes, gentlemen. Wear them like I'm wearing mine." The prophet adjusted his so that it sat at the proper angle. "Please accept this yoke as a gift from Yahweh to your king." He laid one in Zedekiah's lap. "Yahweh says: 'I made the earth, the sea, the heavens, and every beast in them. I have the power to do whatever I wish with all these things, and to give them to whomever I choose.

"'I have given the earth and everyone on it to Nebuchadnezzar and his successors. All nations will serve him. Someday I will destroy Babylon, but until then, every nation who refuses to submit to its yoke will die by sword, famine, and pestilence. Yet those who wear Babylon's yoke will remain in their own lands.

"'Do not listen to anyone who tells you to resist, for I have spoken,' says Yahweh, 'and I will cause it to happen.'"

"These will make interesting souvenirs," the Ammonite envoy sneered after Jeremiah had left the room. "But I have no intention of serving Babylon all my life."

"Nor do I," Zedekiah agreed as he contemptuously tossed the wooden yoke into a corner.

"Let us form an alliance against Babylon," the Ammonite announced as he broke the yoke over his knee.

Chapter 12

Traitor! Stop Him!

"We can achieve victory only if the gods direct this war," Nebuchadnezzar told his chamberlain.

The royal cupbearer bowed before the king. "I've already summoned the astrologers and soothsayers, your majesty."

"Good." The Babylonian king paced around his chariot, stopping at times to pat the side of one of his white stallions as he studied the distant horizon. He had halted his army at a fork in the road—one trail led south to Jerusalem, while the other stretched westward toward Tyre and Sidon. The king had launched this campaign for the purpose of putting an end to the revolt that Zedekiah began when he followed the counsel of the ambassadors, but this course could be disastrous if the gods had decreed something else. Nebuchadnezzar sought their will several times already, but he wanted to be sure.

"Your advisors have arrived, your majesty," the chamberlain announced.

"Very well," said Nebuchadnezzar as he turned to address the small group of well-dressed men. These counselors were priests and claimed to have direct access to the gods who controlled Babylon's destiny. All of them carried sacks, filled with the tools of their persuasions, for each one used a different method to discover the will of his god. They seldom brought a unanimous report, but a simple majority was considered sufficient.

"Gentlemen," said the king, "which road shall we take? Shall we go south to Jerusalem, or west to Tyre and Sidon?"

Fire in the Gates

One by one the pagan priests performed their rituals. One killed a kid, removed its liver, and examined it carefully to see what important information the gods wished to reveal. Another whirled a quiver containing pointless arrows around his head until one of the arrows flew out—each arrow had been tagged for identification—and the dislodged arrow revealed the will of his god. A third priest examined an image to discover clues that would tell him the message that his god had sent.

After all the priests had consulted their deities, they brought their report to Nebuchadnezzar—and this time every priest agreed: advance toward Jerusalem, for the gods will grant victory.

Unit leaders shouted commands all down the lines, and the enormous army began to crawl southward—a seething, multinational mass of men who had been drafted to fight for Babylon. The rumble of hundreds of thousands of feet, prancing horse hooves, and chariot and pack wagon wheels could be heard for many miles. On windless days clouds of dust stirred up by this vast horde rose hundreds of feet into the air. Surprise attack was impossible with such an army, but Nebuchadnezzar didn't mind. No city or nation could resist him anyway.

Within weeks the Babylonian army surrounded Jerusalem, set up camp, and prepared for a long siege. Scouts studied the gates and the walls that bristled with thousands of armed defenders. As the sun set over Mount Zion, soldiers prepared for the night and then gathered into campfire groups to joke and discuss the coming siege.

At dawn the massive war machine cranked into action. They did not surge into a headlong assault of the towering walls, but merely began building siege devices that would aid them in weakening the defenders and breaking down the city walls. Their greatest task lay in building mounds against the wall—ramps to be used by the crews who operated the battering rams, and then later by the infantry during its final charge over the top. The soldiers built these mounds, abandoning their shields and spears—their swords remained strapped to their sides—to tote baskets of dirt and rocks from the hills and valleys around Jerusalem.

Others felled every tree in sight and stacked the logs near the city for use in the ramps and for the construction of siege machines. Engineers fabricated towers from which archers could rain arrows down upon the city; catapults that would hurl rocks over the wall to destroy houses and kill people; and battering rams to break down the upper portion of the wall in preparation for the final assault.

While the main force prepared for the siege, Nebuchadnezzar ordered his veteran platoons into the country-side to capture the walled villages and the numerous un-protected towns.

🔥 🔥 🔥

The citizens of Jerusalem quaked at the sight of Babylonian hordes surrounding their city. They recognized that only a few months separated them from defeat or death. Everyone knew that Zedekiah was no Hezekiah and had made few preparations for the siege. The food warehouses stood half empty, and much of the available grain had already spoiled. Few had bothered to fill any of the cisterns, and most of those that did contain water stank from the putrid remains of in-sects, rats, and an occasional dog or cat. No one had cleaned Hezekiah's tunnel for years, and the system which had been designed to bring fresh drinking water to thirsty people now often carried raw sewage.

Zedekiah couldn't have been less concerned over condi-tions. In the rest of the city, palace supplies of food and water had been kept in good order. "The Babylonians are only bluffing," he announced to his counselors. "They'll soon weary of trying to break through these impregnable walls and go somewhere else." He had no idea of Nebuchadnezzar's persistence. (The Babylonian king spent 13 years besieging the city of Tyre before destroying it.) So life in Jerusalem continued almost as though no enemy surrounded its walls.

🔥 🔥 🔥

During the reigns of Jehoiakim and Zedekiah, the upper class had enslaved their poor fellow Judahites through devious means. Wealthy individuals would force the financially distressed into circumstances that made it necessary for them to borrow funds to plant their crops. After a short time the lenders would demand their money at high interest, and, since the paupers had no way of paying it, they and their families had to sell themselves into slavery. (Jewish law allowed for the payment of debts through enforced labor by the man and/or his family when the borrower had no funds with which to repay his debts.)

The laws of Moses required Jewish slaves to receive their freedom after six years. But no one listened to Moses anymore, so the rich refused to free their debt slaves, and the bondage continued for life.

The siege lasted longer than Zedekiah or his counselors had expected, and they began to realize that Nebuchadnezzar actually planned to destroy Jerusalem. Something had to be done, and quickly.

The prime minister made a suggestion one day: "Jeremiah and other prophets have preached for many years that God will curse our nation because the wealthy have enslaved the poor. Perhaps, if we followed their counsel, who knows? Maybe God would save us." The smile on his lips portrayed amusement, but his manner was serious.

Zedekiah vacillated as always. He didn't like the idea of

losing his slaves, but before long his counselors convinced themselves that the gamble might pay off, and, in the end, the king proclaimed the release of: "all Jewish slaves are to be freed, and remain free forever."

The nobility grumbled, but they obeyed. By nightfall every slave had been freed, and the poor thrilled with joy. On the following day, thousands of former slaves joined the army to fight the common enemy.

🔥 🔥 🔥

The siege had gone on for several months, and Jerusalem at last began to feel its impact. Food became scarce, water ran low, and no rationing existed to protect the remaining meager supplies. The wealthy, forced to do their own work, yearned for the return of their slaves. Tempers flared everywhere; fights, thefts, and even murder became commonplace as the fate of the city became more certain.

But as suddenly as the Babylonians had come, they disappeared, with the last stragglers seen streaming toward the north at daybreak one day. Had they quit? Or did they march to some distant war? No one knew. But Jerusalem rejoiced.

The once teeming Babylonian camp lay empty—save for the tons of rubbish that littered the countryside, the siege machines standing quietly where they had been abandoned, the ramps that still disgraced the wall, the charred rocks that dotted the hillsides where thousands of campfires had burned the night before. Crowds of delighted people ventured out of the city to find food and collect anything else of value that the Babylonians might have left behind.

The answer to the riddle arrived by messenger on the following day: Pharaoh Hophra's approach had evidently frightened the Babylonians away. Cheers filled Jerusalem—not for the salvation that Yahweh had provided, or for the thousands of once-enslaved people who now lived as free men, nor for the godly counsel they received daily from Jeremiah and Baruch. No. Instead they all saluted Pharaoh Hophra as the savior of Judah.

Believing that they had been rescued from the Babylonians, the wealthy now reversed the decree that they had agreed to in an attempt to convince God to deliver the city. All those who had been freed—forever, as the decree had stated—were now re-enslaved by their former owners. The joy of freedom quickly evaporated as former slaves again submitted to their masters. The nobility on the other hand, rejoiced at regaining their former ease, while prophets warned of retribution to come and of the certain return of Nebuchadnezzar.

But no one listened.

🔥 🔥 🔥

Jeremiah supposed that he had finished his dual work of warning his people against every vice imaginable and of calling the nation to reform. Since Judah refused to repent and continued to meander down the road to ruin, he decided that he had but one more job to do—he must rescue the ark of the covenant.

Striding into the Temple court, he spoke to the high priest. "Nebuchadnezzar will soon return to destroy Jerusalem and the Temple," he announced. "But we cannot allow the ark to fall into Babylonian hands."

The high priest's nostrils flared, and he clenched his fists at the mention of the destruction of the Temple, but Jeremiah held up his hands. "Remember the first time Nebuchadnezzar came to Jerusalem?"

"Yes," grunted the high priest.

"He didn't destroy the city or the Temple then, but he did take the sacred vessels."

The official priest reluctantly nodded, but he still bristled at Jeremiah's dire prediction about the Temple.

"Whether or not he actually destroys the Temple is not the issue, my friend." Jeremiah said kindly. "When Nebuchadnezzar returns, he will surely remove the rest of the sacred Temple vessels—including the ark of the covenant."

"I see what you mean," the high priest sighed. "What should we do?"

"We must hide the ark where the Babylonians can never find it. Then when the trouble passes, we can return it to the Temple. But if Nebuchadnezzar carries it away to Babylon, we'll never see it again."

"All right. Will you help us?"

"Of course," Jeremiah smiled.

After dark, when the Temple gates had been barred and the streets lay empty, several priests crept quietly through the court and disappeared into the Temple—their white linen garments covered with sackcloth. The high priest, carrying a large cloth, entered the Most Holy Place alone, covered the ark, pulled the veil aside, and whispered to the others to join him. Four men, walking backward so they could not see the interior of the sacred room, grasped the long poles that protruded from the ark and lifted it lovingly from the spot on which it had rested since the days of Solomon.

Silently they passed the golden altar of incense, the table of shewbread on the left and the seven-branched candlestick on the right. From there they tiptoed between the towering bronze pillars on the front of the Temple, down the steps, and into the night. None of them realized that they would never see the sacred ark again.

🔥 🔥 🔥

Jeremiah, though exhausted by the night's work, rejoiced that the ark rested safely from pagan hands. Now he intended to follow his own advice to leave the city. Stopping by his room, he gathered a few belongings and headed for the Sheep Gate at the northeast corner of the city. He decided to go by way of Anathoth, hoping to say goodbye to any friendly relatives who might have gone there after the Babylonian retreat. Then he planned to hike into the hills in search of a safe hiding place.

A smile fluttered over his lips as he contemplated the freedom he would enjoy in the countryside. He had no desire to stay in Jerusalem during the dark days to come, and since his work seemed over, he could rest from his labors and watch the tragedy unfold from a distance.

As the prophet passed through the gate, a startled voice shattered his reverie. "There's a traitor! Stop him!"

Jeremiah looked around to see what unfortunate man the guards would catch, only to see one of them pointing directly at him! He had no chance to react, for strong hands grasped his arms and dragged him toward the guardhouse.

"That's the man," Irijah, one of the sentries proclaimed. "That's Jeremiah, the one who's been telling everyone to leave Jerusalem and surrender to the enemy. I'll bet he's fleeing to Nebuchadnezzar right now."

"Really?" The other guards gawked at the prophet.

"Yes. And he's the one responsible for the death of my grandfather, Hananiah." A smirk played at the corners of his mouth. "Take him to the dungeon underneath the house of Jonathan the secretary. We'll see what becomes of his prophecies of doom."

Chapter 13

A Piece of Ground for a Prisoner

"I'm not a traitor," Jeremiah protested as two guards dragged him back into Jerusalem.

"You're the worst kind," Irijah hissed. "You killed my grandfather by your witchery and spread your seditious lies everywhere. 'My people,'" he mocked. "'Surrender is your only hope!'" He squeezed Jeremiah's arm until it almost cut off the circulation. "'Traitor' is the kindest word for you."

The trio stopped at a door that appeared to be an entrance to the basement of a large building, and Irijah pounded on it with the side of his fist, as though the occupants would ignore an ordinary knock. A loud squeak resounded through the rough planks as someone on the inside slid the wooden bar lock aside. With a creak the door opened, and an armed guard scowled out at them. "You don't have to beat the door down!" he shouted. "What do you want?"

"We bring you the most infamous traitor ever to grace the cells of your prison," Irijah snapped. "Jeremiah, the false prophet." The word 'prophet' sounded as if he had spat it out. "He wants us to surrender."

The frowning guard grunted in response.

"Put him in your most secure cell." Irijah pushed Jeremiah through the door. "Give him water, but no food until further orders. And no visitors."

"With pleasure." The guard grasped Jeremiah's arm and nearly lifted him off his feet. "I'll treat this one like royalty," he grinned, "a captured rebel king." The jailer hustled the prophet down a darkened hallway and shoved him into a vaulted chamber with such force that Jeremiah lost his footing and sprawled onto a moldy pile of straw in the far corner. Two rats scurried for safety as he landed.

Jeremiah stared around at his cell while the jailer barred the door. The rocks comprising the walls fit together so closely that digging through them would be out of the question, and the small hole near the ceiling admitted insufficient light and air. He fought off a wave of nausea brought on by the stench of sweat, urine, and sewage that permeated the room. But the rustle of the rats troubled him even more, for he knew he would have to sleep on their level.

"Baruch won't be allowed to visit me," he mumbled. "He won't even know I'm here, for I told him this morning that l would go to Anathoth and beyond."

He sat on his putrid pile of straw and wept. "O Yahweh," he prayed. "I thought You were finished with me, that I could go away and rest. But now I'm in this awful dungeon. They want to starve me. 'No food,' he said. 'Only water.' Do You have work for me here? Show me what You want me to do, and give me the courage to do it."

The darkness in the cell seemed to recede, the rats became quiet, and his hunger disappeared.

🔥 🔥 🔥

Jeremiah had been in prison for several days when it occurred to him that his situation there had not been as bad as he had anticipated. He hadn't seen any rats since his arrival; the straw seemed softer than most sleeping mats; the air actually smelled fresh; and a soft light brightened the cell, even at night. *Yahweh abides with me, even in this dungeon,* he thought.

The rattle of the door of his cell startled him, and he looked up as two men entered—Pashur, the Temple governor, who had twice persecuted Jeremiah; and Zephaniah, the second-highest priest.

"Jeremiah," Zephaniah spoke first, "we come from King Zedekiah to ask you to pray for Judah."

"That's right," Pashur added, the words clearly distasteful to him. "Nebuchadnezzar has driven off the Egyptian army, and we fear that he will soon return to Jerusalem. Many years ago, when Sennacherib attacked the city, Isaiah prayed, and Yahweh destroyed the Assyrian army. We know that Yahweh listens to your prayers, Jeremiah, so perhaps if you prayed for us, we would be saved too."

"I will gladly pray for Judah," he assured them. "But I cannot pray as Isaiah did, for most of the people obeyed Yahweh then. Today almost everyone worships idols—from the king who sits on the throne to the priests who serve in the Temple. How can Yahweh save a nation of pagans?" He searched the faces of both visitors. "I will pray instead that the people will repent so that Yahweh will be able to save them."

The priests winced at Jeremiah's rebuke and turned to leave. "Tell your master," the prophet called after them, "that Judah will follow his leadership. If he repents, the nation will copy his example, and that will permit Yahweh to save our country."

The door opened, and the men passed through it, and it closed, the heavy bar dropping into place. The sound of footsteps drifted down the hail and faded away. *If I had given a favorable answer,* Jeremiah mused, *I could be strolling, at this minute, in sunlit streets toward the palace, and food!* But he instantly dismissed the thought. "I can speak only what Yahweh tells me to speak, nothing more, nothing less."

Other footsteps soon echoed in the hallway and stopped outside his cell. He heard the bar raised and then the door opened. A uniformed man, wearing the scarlet sash of a palace guard, looked down at the prophet. "The king desires to speak with you."

Fire in the Gates

Jeremiah struggled to his feet and followed without a word, happy if only for a change of scenery. Outside, the sunlight blinded him, and he clung to the soldier's arm for several minutes. When he at last became accustomed to the brightness, he noticed everyone staring at him. *Of course,* he thought. *A disheveled prisoner walking on the arm of a palace guard would cause a sensation.*

When they reached the royal mansion, Jeremiah's escort allowed him time to wash his face, comb his increasingly white hair and beard, and don clean clothes before he entered Zedekiah's presence.

The prophet marveled that the king had changed so much. Once noble in height and attitude, now he stooped and stared through eyes filled with anger, distrust, and indecision. "I'm so glad you've come." The king's tone of sincerity did not match his expression. "Pashur and Zephaniah told me that you would pray for us. That pleases me."

"Do you really think Yahweh can save you as He did Hezekiah?" Jeremiah's voice betrayed his disbelief.

"We can hope, can't we?"

"It takes more than hope," the prophet insisted. "Yahweh demands that you put away your sins before He can work for you. If you refuse, even your prayers will turn His stomach." Jeremiah pointed at the king. "Unless you repent, Zedekiah, God will fight against you and send you to Babylon in chains."

The monarch's eyes widened in terror. He opened his mouth to speak, but no words came. He had guessed that the end approached, but Jeremiah's indictment caused him to tremble.

"We have so little time," the prophet implored. "If you don't want to repent, at least surrender to Babylon and spare the lives of your people."

At last Zedekiah found his voice. "Jeremiah, you—you're asking too much."

"Too much! I'm asking nothing! This is Yahweh's plan to save your life."

"L-let me think about it. I'll talk to you later." He motioned to the guard to take Jeremiah away.

"May I ask one favor?" the prophet said as the soldier grasped his arm. "Don't send me back to the house of Jonathan. They allow me no food. I'll die there."

"Put him in the courtyard prison," Zedekiah told the guard, "and see that he receives food as long as our supplies last."

"Thank you, sir." For the first time in days Jeremiah smiled.

🔥 🔥 🔥

Zedekiah resolved to surrender as Jeremiah had counseled and summoned his staff to announce his decision.

"What!" the prime minister exploded. "Are you out of your mind? Didn't you realize that Jeremiah is being charged with treason?"

"B-but he's telling the truth, I-I know he is." Sweat glistened on Zedekiah's forehead.

"You—." The chief general spat on the floor in disgust. "Who ever heard of asking a prophet about foreign affairs?"

The room rocked with laughter. Zedekiah hated these men, but he feared them too. If he refused their advice, they could dethrone him—or even assassinate him. Torn between truth and duty on the one hand, and powerful, evil men on the other, Zedekiah's decision to obey Yahweh like withered grass before a hot desert wind.

"All right!" he shouted. "Have it your way. But we're all doomed!"

🔥 🔥 🔥

After his long time in the dungeon beneath the house of Jonathan the royal secretary, Jeremiah now felt almost like dancing. Although he'd delivered a message of woe, he had still received a reward for it—the prison in the king's courtyard sported trees, flowers, space for exercise in the sunshine, and food! He still marveled at the turn of events when Baruch's brother called at his cell.

"What brings you to the palace prison, Seraiah?" Jeremiah asked, smiling.

"I heard that you are here." The man's face showed his concern. "Why have they imprisoned you?"

Jeremiah briefly related what had happened. "Isn't it wonderful, Seraiah? What a pleasant place!"

"It's better than that dungeon," he agreed, "but I wish you were free."

"Yahweh has work for me to do here," Jeremiah said. "I'm sure that this bondage has a purpose."

"I will help you all I can. May Yahweh be kind to you."

Baruch arrived the following day. "I had thought that by now you'd be in some far-off cave," he said. "But no one can escape now, for the Babylonians have returned. It's only a matter of time before—" His voice faded away, for he couldn't bring himself to utter the fateful words.

"How true," the prophet acknowledged. He could see the city's defenders gathered on the wall near the Ephraim Gate.

The scribe changed the subject. "A refugee from Anathoth moved in next door to me—one of your cousins—and he tells me of some property for sale near home."

Jeremiah smiled. "I'd like to talk with him."

Later in the day he chatted with his cousin. "It's so good to hear news from home. I haven't been there for many years."

"I know, not since my father and his brothers tried to kill you."

"You knew about that?"

"Everybody did," the man confessed, "but Baruch was

the only one who had the courage to warn you. The rest of us feared we'd risk our necks if we tried to save you. How wrong we were."

"You no longer think that it's better for one man to die than to disturb a nation?"

"It's never right for an innocent man to die, whatever the cause. To do right and to walk humbly before Yahweh—that is the first and best duty of man." Jeremiah could tell from the expression in his cousin's eyes that he believed what he had said.

Resting his hand on the man's shoulder, Jeremiah smiled. "Baruch tells me that you know of land for sale in Anathoth."

"Yes. I came to Jerusalem to see if you wanted to buy it, for you are a closer relative of the man who died than I. You should have the first option to buy it." The man glanced at the Mount of Olives, now crawling with enemy troops. "It looks as though I'm stuck here now until the Babylonians leave."

"Have you seen the land?"

"Oh, yes. It lies south of Anathoth, down by the old fig grove. The boundary runs along the grove for about 50 cubits, then west over the top of the hill for 75 cubits, north to the stone marker, and east again to the grove. It would be a fine place for a vineyard."

"I know the spot, and it is a fine field. Will you buy it if I don't?"

"By all means!"

"I can see that your heart is set on it," Jeremiah sighed, "but I will buy the land myself."

"But you're in prison," the cousin protested, "and we're surrounded by the enemy. You can't even go out to look it over."

"I don't need to. You have examined it, and I trust you. Yes, I intend to buy it for myself."

"But you said that the Babylonians would conquer Jerusalem this time," Baruch, who had been listening quietly now objected. "How will you ever use it?"

"Our people will go into captivity, but many will return to build and plant again." Jeremiah's gaze narrowed as he spoke. "What better way to teach this lesson than to buy land near Anathoth. Now, Baruch," he pointed toward the prison gate, "bring the necessary papers and witnesses so we can make the transaction. Oh, yes, and stop by the Temple to pick up my priest allowance before you return."

Baruch composed the deed, found witnesses to verify the sale, fetched Jeremiah's pay, and took them all to the prison.

A small crowd gathered to observe the odd transaction. People questioned each other why the prophet would buy a field while living in prison and preaching that Babylon would carry everyone to captivity.

So Jeremiah explained his actions before he took the judicial oath in the presence of the witnesses. He then had the treasurer weigh out 17 shekels (a unit of weight) in silver pieces on his scales—the price of an ox or about nine sheep. After this he affixed his signature to the documents by rolling his signet seal in a ball of clay over the knot of the string tying the deed shut.

"Baruch," Jeremiah instructed his scribe, "place these documents in an earthen jar and seal it so that neither weather, nor rats, nor insects can destroy them." He studied the enemy troops milling around on the Mount of Olives. "After the captivity, either I, or one of my relatives, will find the deed and use the field."

Chapter 14

Chest-deep in Mud

"Of all the nerve!" Pashur exploded. "Jeremiah almost persuaded the king to surrender!"

"He did, at that," agreed Gedaliah, Pashur's son, "and if Zedekiah hadn't told us about it, we'd be marching to Babylon right now."

"No!" Shephatiah countered. "We'd be dead." He scowled beneath his thick eyebrows. "We're the nation's leaders, remember? Whether they capture us or we surrender, it makes no difference. Our heads will roll."

"They'll roll if we're lucky," Jucal said. "They'll probably torture us to death." He shivered at the thought of the unspeakable agonies the Babylonians were known to wreak upon their victims.

"We've got to stop Jeremiah." Pashur fought to control his anger. "He's troubled us at the Temple for years, and now he's deceived the king."

"And it will happen again," Shephatiah added. "Zedekiah will listen to his lies, and next time he may surrender without telling us. You can't trust the king to stick by his decisions any longer than it takes him to consult some other adviser."

"Jeremiah is under arrest, isn't he?" Jucal said quietly.

"Yes," the others chorused.

"What is the punishment for treason?" Jucal continued.

"Death," Gedaliah answered.

"We're all judges." Jucal glanced at each man in turn.

"So why don't we pronounce judgment upon him and then execute him?"

They all knew that, according to divine law, their plan would amount to murder, but their hatred of Jeremiah led them to ignore the whisperings of conscience.

Pashur's grin melted into a frown. "Jeremiah is in the king's prison. Won't we need Zedekiah's permission to execute him?"

"Of course," Shephatiah replied, "but he always does whatever we suggest. He'll give Jeremiah to us."

The four officials waited several days before making their request.

"Your majesty." Pashur bowed to show his respect. "A problem has come to our attention that only you can solve. A man is in your prison who has been judged guilty of treason. Now, sir, if you allow this man to live, you not only break the law, but you also demoralize our people."

"Really?" The king's eyes widened. "Who is he?"

"Jeremiah," Pashur said softly.

"Jeremiah! Treason?" The king leaped to his feet. "He's no traitor, and you know it! I've allowed you to have him held, but this is too much!"

"But, your majesty." Jucal fought to remain calm and not become the target of Zedekiah's anger. "The courts have examined the charges produced by the royal guard Irijah and others, and have found Jeremiah guilty of persuading our people to desert to the enemy. Many have followed his advice and even now fight against us."

"Preposterous!" The king stomped down the steps leading to his throne and shook his fist in Jucal's face. "You devised this little scheme because you hate him! I won't let you do it!"

"We're sorry you feel that way, your majesty." Pashur bowed again. "But when you harbor a condemned criminal, you become a coconspirator."

"You snakes," Zedekiah hissed. "You always twist things to suit your own ends."

"Our ways are the ways of justice," Pashur said quietly.

"Treacherous injustice!" Zedekiah spat out the words. "Out of here, you rats! Get out!"

"Sir," Pashur persisted, "we must have Jeremiah, or the city will rebel against you."

"Take him!" the king screamed. "Take him, and get out of my sight. I hate you all!" The king grabbed a spear from a nearby guard and hurled it at the retreating men, failing to notice that he had flung it backwards. The blunt end struck Shephatiah in the side, but damaged little more than his pride.

Once outside, the men scurried toward the prison. "We must act quickly," Jucal whispered. "Zedekiah may change his mind."

"If the king were a warrior, I'd be dead," Shephatiah gasped, flinching as he touched his bruises.

"You would," Gedaliah agreed, as he motioned for the group to stop. "Listen. Many people sympathize with Jeremiah, and if we execute him publicly, we risk starting a riot." He paused and stared toward the prison gate, deep in thought. "But if he were to die in an accident . . ."

"Good thinking, my son," Pashur said, after a moment's thought. "And I think I know how to do it."

"How?" chorused the group.

"Many years ago Malchiah dug a cistern in the prison court, but it leaked and held only enough water to create mud."

They divided to carry out their plan. Pashur and Gedaliah entered the prison and ambled toward the row of cells opposite Jeremiah's, so the guards wouldn't suspect them later.

A few minutes later, Jucal and Shephatiah strolled into the prison guardhouse. The two men stood idly talking to the bored guards so that the soldiers' backs would be turned toward the court.

Meanwhile, Pashur and Gedaliah, their hands over Jeremiah's mouth, dragged the protesting prophet toward the cistern, from which they had already removed the lid. They tied a rope around his waist and shoved him down in the opening. Jeremiah clung to the sides of the hole, but Pashur stamped on his fingers, and then lowered the protesting prophet to the bottom, where he sank up to his chest in the smelly slime. The depths of the cistern muffled his howls.

When Jucal and Shephatiah finished chatting with the guards, they entered the prison to see one of the inmates. While crossing the courtyard, they "discovered" that the cistern lid was off and ignored the pitiful pleas of Jeremiah as they replaced it. After their brief visit with one of the prisoners, they returned to the guardhouse.

"You should be more careful," Jucal chided the guards a few minutes later. "We found the cistern lid off. Could be dangerous, you know. Someone might fall into it."

The guard shot a glance at the courtyard. "I didn't know it was off!" His shock dissolved into relief when he saw that it was back on again. "Thanks for replacing it." He grimaced. "We'll try to be more careful."

🔥 🔥 🔥

Jeremiah shouted until his voice grew hoarse, but no one could hear him. Although he wasn't seriously hurt, the mud chilled him to the marrow. He considered his peril—sunk up to his armpits in mud. Even if he could extricate himself from the mud, he couldn't reach the opening and its lid. And even if he could reach them, he wouldn't have the strength to lift the covering by himself.

"If no one rescues me soon," he moaned, "I'll die. O Yahweh, save me!" he prayed in desperation.

At that moment the palace eunuch and his aide strode

through the prison gate in search of Jeremiah. Ebed-Melech, a Black man from the land of Cush, held a high office in the government, and when he did not find the prophet in his cell, he stood before it for a moment rubbing his whiskerless chin.

"Perhaps he's visiting with another prisoner," his aide suggested.

But as they passed from cell to cell, calling the prophet's name, they discovered that no one had seen him—until they inquired at the cell farthest from the gate.

"Jeremiah?" the prisoner said. "I saw two of the noblemen talking with him over by the cistern about two hours ago. I didn't see what they were doing or where they went after that."

"The cistern?" Ebed-Melech's pulse pounded in his throat. He knew of the hatred many of the nobility had for Jeremiah, because he had overheard them arguing with the king earlier that day. His mind whirled as he mentally put the puzzle together.

"Those devils!" he hissed as he turned on his heel and raced toward the cistern. He stopped directly over the lid, lifted it with one mighty heave, and then called into the black hole. "Jeremiah? Jeremiah!"

"Here I am," the prophet hoarsely replied. "Ebed-Melech? Is th-that you? P-please get me out of here. I'll d-die down here."

The eunuch knew that his friend needed help, and that only Zedekiah could authorize it. His anger burned at the callousness of men who could kill an old man in such a cruel, lingering way.

"Hold on, Jeremiah," he shouted. "I'll get you out."

Leaving his aide to guard the cistern, Ebed-Melech raced across the courtyard, through the guardhouse (he ignored the guards), out of the palace, around the east end of the Temple, and down the street toward the East Gate, where the king sat in court as the judge of the city.

The monarch was engrossed in a legal debate when the eunuch puffed to a stop before him, but Ebed-Melech couldn't wait until the trial's end. Springing to the front, he bowed before the king. "Your majesty," he panted, "excuse my intrusion, but I must speak to you about a matter of life or death."

"Very well," the king responded, curious at the sudden interruption. "Court stands adjourned until I return."

The two men entered a nearby guardhouse. "Sir," began Ebed-Melech still breathing hard, "you did an evil thing when you gave those noblemen license to treat Jeremiah as they pleased. Do you know what they did?"

"No." The king almost choked on his own guilt.

"They put him down Malchiah's cistern. He's sunk into the mud up to his armpits." Tears filled the eunuch's eyes. "Sir, he'll die down there if we don't get him out."

"You are more righteous than I." The king could scarcely speak above a whisper. "All right, take 30 soldiers—in case the nobles give you any trouble. Get Jeremiah out of there. I-I won't let this happen again."

"Thank you, sir." The eunuch bowed and departed.

Ebed-Melech drafted 30 palace guards to help him. "I don't think the nobles will bother us," he said, after he had briefed them, "but be alert." He ordered two men to fetch a stout rope, two more to find rags for cushioning, and others to secure food, water, and new clothing for Jeremiah, while he led the rest of them to the cistern.

Immediately Ebed-Melech lay face down on the ground and stuck his head into the cistern opening. "Are you still alive, my friend?"

"Yes, sir," Jeremiah answered, "but I c-couldn't last a full d-day down here." He shivered as he spoke. "It's so c-cold and damp. All my b-bones hurt."

"We'll have you out soon. My men are bringing a rope."

A few minutes later Ebed-Melech tied a loop at the end of the rope and lowered it to Jeremiah. "Put this loop just under your armpits." He tossed down the rags. "And tuck these under the rope so it won't chafe your skin."

The men tugged on the rope. Although Jeremiah didn't weigh much, the mud held him. At last the slime released him with a slurping sound, and he rose to ground level.

The men stripped off his wet, muddy clothes, bathed and dressed him in clean, dry garments, and fed him the best food he'd tasted in many days.

"Ebed-Melech." Jeremiah's tongue seemed to caress the name. "You and all your men treated me like a son. Yahweh has this to say to you. 'Soon Jerusalem will fall, and thousands will die in the slaughter; but God will spare your lives because you have shown love to one of Yahweh's servants.'"

"Yahweh is merciful," the eunuch breathed. "May He be praised for all His blessings."

Chapter 15

Last Chance for Life

"Look at those siege towers," Baruch said as he and Jeremiah watched the barrage of enemy arrows darkening the sky over the nearby Ephraim Gate.

"Yes, Baruch," Jeremiah stroked his white beard. "And unless Zedekiah surrenders soon, most of our people will die."

"Is there no hope?"

"Not unless Zedekiah surrenders." The prophet pushed a stone with his foot and then dragged it back again. "If he would surrender, no one else would die."

"Why doesn't he?"

Jeremiah studied the Babylonian archers on the siege tower for a long time before answering. "He has rebelled against God all his life and repeatedly announced that Yahweh has no power to protect Judah. In fact he has gone even so far as to say that he would never serve the Lord as long as he lived. Time and again he has convinced the people that resistance to Babylon would mean survival. Remember? He said it just the other day. 'Surrender shows cowardice.' I think he's repeated that phrase so often that he believes it himself. Would you expect him to give in now? No, he would consider it a sign of weakness. I think he fears public opinion here in Jerusalem far more than he does the Babylonian army out there."

"And his fears will kill the city."

"That's right." Jeremiah sighed and his eyes filled with tears, his voice choked with emotion. "And he won't escape, either."

"What will happen to him?"

"He will—" The prophet stopped when he heard footsteps.

"Jeremiah!" an approaching guard called. "Come with me."

"Who wants to see me?"

"I cannot tell you, sir, but do come quickly."

Jeremiah turned to Baruch. "I'll see you tomorrow, I hope. Your visits brighten my days."

"I'll come," Baruch said over his shoulder as he headed toward the prison gate.

🔥 🔥 🔥

Jeremiah studied the intricate patterns of flowers and leaves painted on the plastered walls of the small palace room. The carved furniture and doorjambs blended with the mosaic tile floor to complete the elegance of the scene. He mentally compared the splendor of this tiny room with the drab gray-plastered dwellings of the common people, but his thoughts froze as the door opened.

"No one must know that we have talked," Zedekiah said as he shut the door and lowered the bar to secure it. "I have some urgent matters to discuss with you privately."

"I do not wish to talk with you! If I tell you the truth, you will only send someone to kill me, just as you did before."

"I didn't send anyone to kill you," the king wheezed, backing away.

"You gave them your permission!"

Zedekiah blushed. "Y-yes I did." He rubbed his hands together nervously. "But I also ordered Ebed-Melech to save you, and I'm glad he did."

"Are you? Really?"

"Why yes, Jeremiah, I need your counsel." The king

brushed his robes as if to rub off any guilt he had incurred from the cistern affair. "But I don't dare let anyone know that I've talked with a prisoner. The royal dignity."

"I'm not interested in your dignity," Jeremiah growled as he turned toward the door.

"Wait, Jeremiah! Please." The king fell on his face as if he were a slave begging for his life. "Don't go!"

The prophet stopped, still facing the door, ignoring the prone royal figure behind him. "I won't talk with you unless you promise me that you won't kill me yourself or permit anyone else to try."

"You have my word," the king assured him, rising to his knees. "I will protect you as long as I have the power to do so."

"All right." Jeremiah turned as the king struggled to his feet. "What do you want to discuss?"

"What will happen to us? Will we all die?"

Jeremiah strolled to the window and gazed into the garden. He stared past the exotic trees and flowers to the siege towers that overlooked the walls. "Thus says Yahweh." His voice sounded like a funeral dirge. "'Behold, I will give this city to the king of Babylon, and he will burn it with fire. You will not escape out of his hand, Zedekiah. He will capture you, and your eyes will see Nebuchadnezzar's eyes. He will speak to you mouth to mouth, and you will go to Babylon.'"

Jeremiah turned toward the king, a slight smile of amazement playing on his lips. "Yet hear the word of Yahweh, O Zedekiah. 'You shall not die by the sword, but you shall die in peace.' And yet," pleaded the prophet, "if you will only surrender, your family will live, and the city will not die."

Zedekiah sank onto a stool, staring wide-eyed, like one who had seen a ghost. Paralyzed with fear, he sat amid beauty, but his mind's eye viewed only chaos. "This city, this palace, the Temple—burned with fire?" His voice choked, as though fearful of uttering blasphemy. "But the gates,

Jeremiah. The gates are too strong! How can they get through those massive gates?"

"Oh, king," Jeremiah pointed out the window, "those gates will burn with fire, and you will know God's anger at your treachery."

"Fire in the gates? Those giant gates? Burn with fire? How can it be?" The king wrung his hands.

"God will do it through Nebuchadnezzar. But, your majesty, none of this need happen. It's up to you. You hold the key to Jerusalem's future. If you surrender, the city will live. Don't you understand that?"

"Y-y-yes," the terrified king stuttered. "B-but I'm afraid. Those of our people already captured by the Babylonians—they'll kill me if I surrender."

"They won't touch you!" Jeremiah shouted in frustration. "If Yahweh can deliver you from your enemies, He can surely save you from your friends."

"I-I guess so." The king rose and paced the floor for several minutes. "But you don't understand, Jeremiah. My policies—how can I change them without losing face? I've always resisted Babylon. If I suddenly surrender, what will my people think?"

"I don't know. But Yahweh says you must, and He will show you what to do and help you do it if you will only decide to follow His will."

"I'll have to think about it." The king seemed to regain his composure. "Go back to the prison, and I'll call for you when I need you."

"Time is vital, your majesty," the prophet stressed. "Every day that you delay, hundreds of people will die. And soon the enemy will break through the walls. You need to decide right away."

"I'll try." The king shrugged, unbarred the door, and left the room.

Chapter 16

Retribution

"Two women just tried to kill me!" Baruch gasped as he slumped down onto the stone bench outside Jeremiah's cell. "I barely escaped with my life." His hands trembled.

"What happened?" Jeremiah sat down beside his friend and put an arm around his shaking shoulders.

"I came upon these two women—over by the Valley Gate—who were carving up the body of a dead child." The scribe stared wildly into space. "Jeremiah, they were eating it raw!" He bowed his head between his knees to stave off his nausea.

After several minutes he straightened up. "I-I couldn't believe it." He looked at Jeremiah, his mouth hanging open for a full minute before he spoke again. "I tried to pull one woman away from the body. 'Don't do such an evil thing,' I said. 'Trust in Yahweh and He will preserve you.' Jeremiah, her eyes—she was wild! The other woman, too. I felt afraid and turned to leave, but both women jumped at me. They grabbed at my arms and stabbed at me with their knives. If I hadn't been stronger than them, they'd be eating me now!"

"That was close," Jeremiah said as he examined the bloody fingerprints on Baruch's tunic. "I'm glad you escaped. But what you saw is happening all over the city." It was Jeremiah's turn to bury his face in his hands. "It's all because our people have turned their backs on their Maker."

"Zedekiah may be king," Baruch growled, the color returning to his cheeks, "but I'm sure he's hungry like the rest of us. The city has no food anywhere for more than a month." He pressed his hand against his shrunken stomach.

"He must still have some food," Jeremiah sighed. "The guards bring me a few crumbs of bread every day."

"They do? Imagine the riot if the people knew that."

Death hung over the city. The air reeked with the stench of raw sewage and rotting corpses. Thousands of bodies lay unburied. The heat felt suffocating, for breezes had not stirred the air for days, and the sun glared down through cloudless summer skies. People's skin, darkened because of hunger and heat, often cracked open and developed oozing sores. Disease had become even more rampant because of the unsanitary conditions. Jeremiah knew that illness had also broken out among the besieging Babylonians. Siege warfare was always a race as to whom would die from sickness first—the people in the besieged city or the armies surrounding it.

The soldiers fighting on the walls suffered even more. They not only starved for food and had no shade to protect them from the blistering sun, but they still had to repel the countless enemy attacks. Many simply dropped dead of exhaustion.

🔥 🔥 🔥

When Zedekiah realized that the enemy would storm the walls within a few hours, he began to panic. The Babylonians had been pounding their battering ram against the wall day and night for many weeks, and all could see that before long the upper part of the wall near the Ephraim Gate would collapse. "Jeremiah says that I'll be captured," the king complained to an aide, "but we'll see about that. I'm slipping out of Jerusalem tonight, and that old Babylonian lion out there can't stop me either."

"You must be crazy," his chief general growled when Zedekiah explained his scheme late that night. "We're surrounded."

Fire in the Gates

"We can do it," the king assured him, pointing to a rough map scratched on a slab of limestone. "The enemy has concentrated his forces here on the north and over there on the west side. It seems that he's ignored the Gate Between the Walls near the pool of Siloam. He has only a half dozen guards down there. If we surprise them without raising an alarm, we can follow the road down to Jericho, cross the Jordan by morning, and then hide somewhere in the hills beyond the river. They'll never find us there."

"Hmmm," the general muttered, amazed at the king's newfound air of authority. "Sounds like it might work at that. When do we start?"

"As soon as we can get a force together. There's no moon tonight." He smiled as he rose from his throne, encouraged now that he had discovered a way to escape. "Pick your strongest men, dress them in black, and explain our plan. This will be our last desperate effort to save the throne."

Within an hour the king's garden, near the old pool, teemed with life as several hundred black-clad, fully-armed soldiers quietly prepared to dash for freedom. Zedekiah and his family joined them about midnight.

Suddenly a cry sounded from the direction of the Ephraim Gate: "The wall is breached! The wall is breached!"

"Let's go!" Zedekiah ordered in a loud whisper, and the men surged toward the Gate Between the Walls.

A watchman on the wall above the gate signaled "all clear." The escape party sallied forth, as advance guards sought out and killed every enemy soldier who stood in their path.

Moving stealthily into the night, Zedekiah felt the pounding of his own heart, as panic constricted his chest, making it difficult for him to breathe.

Why should I run like this? he thought. *I must be mad to fight against Yahweh. But still, I can't see any point being killed in Jerusalem. I have to run. I want to live!*

The Kidron Valley seemed deserted as they hurried southward. Jerusalem disappeared behind the silhouette of a hill, but no one followed them. They crossed another ridge and then another. Still no sign of enemy pursuit.

"Faster," Zedekiah whispered to his general. "I think we've left them behind."

The platoon lurched into a gallop, still cautious lest they stumble onto an enemy patrol, yet longing for the light of morning and the sight of the Jordan River. Zedekiah uttered occasional words of encouragement to a wife or a son as the refugees emerged from the central hills and followed the road that plunged toward the Dead Sea valley.

As dawn climbed the sky, a soldier in the rear shouted, "Enemy in pursuit!"

Zedekiah whirled in his saddle, his heart leaping into his throat. He could see from the size of the dust clouds behind them that the Babylonian forces were moving faster, and greatly outnumbered his own. They would soon overtake him.

"Hurry!" he cried, sweeping his hand in a wide arch toward the distant horizon. "Ride for Jordan!"

The men spurred their horses, but with no prearranged plan, they galloped off in all directions at once. A few of his closest bodyguards, his wives, and his three sons were all that remained with the king.

"Come back, you cowards!" Zedekiah screamed as he stood in his saddle. "Come back, I say!"

It was no use. Within seconds he rode virtually alone and helpless. "Let's go," he shouted, whipping his horse. But the race ended almost before it had begun, for Zedekiah's mounts were nearly dead from starvation and fatigue.

Nebuchadnezzar's patrols caught up with and surrounded him within sight of the Jordan. After giving Zedekiah some food and water, they chained him behind the captor's horse for the 20-mile trip back to Jerusalem. Only his wives were allowed to ride. "Jeremiah was right," he moaned to himself. "If only I had listened. If only—"

🔥 🔥 🔥

On the morning of the assault, Baruch stayed with Jeremiah in the prison. When the sky began to lighten above the Mount of Olives the two wandered to the southwest end of the courtyard to watch the fighting near the Ephraim Gate.

Cascades of arrows crisscrossed between the siege tower and the city's defenders. Scores of men fell wounded and dying on both sides as the battle intensified. Fighting had centered around the breach in the wall for hours, but now walkways emerged from the tower, reaching the top of the wall. The brave defenders who sprang forward to dislodge them died in the hail of arrows, as did the first Babylonians who sought to cross.

Jeremiah's eyes welled with tears. "If only Zedekiah had surrendered," he kept repeating, "all those people would not be dying."

Hundreds perished in the final struggle. The Babylonian forces poured through the openings in the wall, and those attempting to cross the bridge from the siege tower were beginning to reach the wall before being cut down by arrows. Within minutes defender and invader fought hand to hand on the wall, the enemy growing in numbers until no defenders remained alive. A cheer reverberated through the air as the hordes poured over the bridge, into the city.

"We'd better get back to my cell," Jeremiah urged as he took hold of Baruch's arm. "We'll be safer there."

The two watched through the hole in the cell door. "We'll survive," the prophet said after a while. "Yahweh promised to spare us, but we must let Him act according to His will."

Baruch sat down on a stool and leaned against the wall. "Zedekiah and his bodyguard escaped last night."

"Really?" Jeremiah still gazed through the tiny window. "They won't get far. Who told you?"

"One of the watchmen down near the Pool of Siloam. They left just after the enemy broke through the Ephraim Wall." The scribe looked up at Jeremiah and sighed. "He caused all this suffering, and now he escapes. I'm really embarrassed to be called his subject." Wiping his eyes with the back of his hand, he said, "Oh, the shame, Jeremiah! I'm not sure I care to survive, what with the nation dying like this."

Shouting came from the courtyard, and Jeremiah peered out. Prison guards fought hand-to-hand with enemy soldiers, but the skirmish lasted only seconds. Jeremiah winced as he saw his friends fall, mortally wounded.

The Babylonians fanned out through the courtyard, wary of further resistance, but when they soon discovered that they had entered a prison, they relaxed. They busied themselves by lining up the prisoners for their evacuation from Jerusalem.

"Do whatever they ask," Jeremiah told Baruch as they joined the others. "They won't harm us now."

After two days of forced marching, Zedekiah and his bone-weary fellows gazed mournfully at the remains of their once beautiful capital city. The walls had collapsed in several places, and more rotting corpses filled the air with a nauseating stench. Even the captors seemed revolted by the mess and led the prisoners northward, seeking a more suitable place to spend the night.

Dawn came again and Zedekiah's group continued their journey. The iron collar had turned his neck into one large, oozing sore, radiating excruciating pain with every movement. His hands were bound behind his back, so he had no way of swatting the flies and other insects that crawled across his bloody wounds. A chain fastened to the lead horse in front of him ran through a loop on his metal collar, and continued on to the prisoners behind him. Their captors had confiscated their sandals, so Zedekiah and his party trudged the hot, rocky road on well-blistered feet.

The tortured men could cover only eight to 10 miles a day, and plodded for an agonizing 18 days before reaching Nebuchadnezzar's headquarters in Riblah, far north of Jerusalem. More than half of the Jewish captives had died during the forced march, and their lifeless bodies had been abandoned to decay in the blazing sun.

Nebuchadnezzar, a muscular man in his late 30s, went into a rage when he saw Zedekiah. "You swore in Yahweh's name that you would serve me faithfully," he swore. He gritted his teeth as he spoke. "Daniel would have kept his word, and I thought you would too."

"I know that Jeremiah warned you to surrender several times," the Babylonian king continued, and Zedekiah marveled at his knowledge of Judahite internal affairs. "But you wouldn't listen to him. And you knew he was innocent of all charges, but you still kept him in prison. Some judge you turned out to be!"

Nebuchadnezzar shook his fist in the captive king's face. "You've caused me a great deal of trouble and have destroyed your own people. You deserve to die!"

The executioners moved toward Zedekiah, but Nebuchadnezzar waved them back. "You dog!" he spat in Zedekiah's face. "Before I get through with you, you'll wish a thousand times that you were dead."

The great king spoke briefly to his chief executioner and then turned again to scowl at Zedekiah. "Take a good look at the results of your rebellion. You may begin," he announced over his shoulder.

Horrified, Zedekiah watched as the executioners selected several Jewish leaders and made them kneel, hands bound behind their backs, heads lowered to expose the nape of the neck. Moving from one to another, the Babylonian raised his sword, and, with one quick, downward stroke, he severed the head from the body. The head tumbled into the dust, an expression of surprise in the still-open, unseeing eyes. The body remained kneeling for several moments before slowly rolling over onto its side.

One by one the leaders died: Seraiah, the chief priest (not Baruch's brother); Zephaniah, the second priest (not the prophet); three priests who had been in charge of the Temple doors; an officer of Zedekiah's army; five royal counselors; Zedekiah's chief scribe; and 60 men who had encouraged the king's rebellion.

All the bloodletting numbed Zedekiah, but he wept aloud when they led his three sons to the death area. "No! No!" he screamed. "Not my sons!" A guard struck him in the face, and he stared in anguish as each young man knelt and lost his head!

"Kill me! Kill me!" Zedekiah wailed as the king's punisher approached him. *Now it's my turn,* he thought. *Soon it will all be over, and peace will come at last—*

But the executioner wiped his sword clean and shoved it into its scabbard. Then with one hand be grabbed Zedekiah's beard, and with the forefinger of the other he gouged out the king's eyes—first one, then the other—as the royal captive howled in pain.

"Take him to Babylon," Nebuchadnezzar shouted. "Let him remember his retribution till the day he dies."

Chapter 17

Free at Last

"Where are they taking us?" a white-haired man in his late 50s asked as he shuffled along in chains with a large group of captives.

"To Ramah," returned his nearest companion. "I heard one of the guards say last night that they'll keep us there for a few days before they send us on to Babylon."

"Good," the first man sighed as he arched his back to relieve some of his pain. "Ramah's not far. We should reach it by sunset." They moved along in silence for some time before he spoke again. "I'm a little old to travel to Babylon on foot. I hope they don't hurry us along too fast."

"Me too," his companion said as he looked intently at his new friend. "Say, aren't you Jeremiah, the prophet?"

"Yes."

"Of course. I've heard you preach dozens of times. I always thought you were senile, or maybe even crazy." He laughed, but then sobered. "I guess you were telling the truth."

"It's not too late to trust in Yahweh," Jeremiah encouraged. "You need Him now, more than ever before."

"I-I guess you're right." He scratched his head and wiped a tear from his cheek as he hung his head. "May Yahweh have mercy upon me and grant me pardon."

Jeremiah smiled to himself as they marched into the gathering twilight—thousands of prisoners shackled together by their necks, walking as carefully as possible so that the neck collars wouldn't chafe the skin more than necessary. The caravan reached Ramah and slowed to a halt. Armed men inspected each prisoner's chain, gave him or her a few morsels of food, a cup of water, and orders to sleep beside the road.

"We captured Jerusalem a month ago," Nebuchadnezzar told Nebuzaradan, the captain of his bodyguard. The king sat on his portable throne in Riblah. "But many people still dwell in the ruins. I'm worried about that city. Its inhabitants could rebuild it and rebel once more. History has repeatedly proved them capable of that." He sat staring at the distant hills. "I don't like it at all," he sighed aloud.

"Can I do anything to be of service?" the captain offered.

The two men discussed various solutions for several hours before the king decided on a plan, and called in a scribe to record it. He gave detailed instructions on what should be done with the people still living in the ruins, how to dismantle the city, when to transport the captives held in Ramah, and many other important items. Nebuzaradan took the king's orders, mustered several thousand soldiers, and embarked, reaching Jerusalem in only 10 days.

There he found found the situation much as Nebuchadnezzar had feared. Except for the breaches made by the battering rams, the siege ramps, and extensive minor damage, the city stood virtually intact. "A well-organized warlord could rebuild Jerusalem in a matter of weeks," the captain commented to one of his orderlies.

The Babylonians went to work, killing anyone who resisted them and rounding up everyone else for the march to Ramah, and later to Babylon. Then they carefully removed every item of value and dismantled the city: They pried apart the stone walls and buildings, set fire to the wooden ones, and piled brush against the massive cedar gates of the Temple, burning them to ashes. The cursing of the soldiers and the thick, black smoke constantly filled the air.

When Nebuzaradan's men finished their work, little remained where Jerusalem had once stood. A traveler would have had difficulty finding shelter from the rain.

The glorious Temple of Solomon lay in heaps of rubble. The scarlet palace built by Jehoiakim at such extravagant expense in money and human lives had become a pile of graywhite powder.

Jerusalem was dead.

Nebuzaradan sent all the valuables found in Jerusalem directly to Babylon and headed for Ramah to deal with the captives. But they numbered far fewer than he'd expected.

"My men have treated the prisoners well," the chief guard assured him as they toured the camp. "Only a relative few have died since they left Jerusalem, and those were in very poor shape when they arrived here."

"Then why so few?" the captain demanded. "Jerusalem must have held a hundred thousand people."

"Few survived the siege. You ought to know that. Half of the people died of starvation or disease before the end, and our soldiers must have killed nearly half of the survivors during the final battle."

"Yes, I guess there's nothing we can do about it now." Nebuzaradan dismissed the matter. "Do you have any prisoners well enough to march?"

"Of course. I'll have my men form a marching party to leave at dawn."

"Good. I'd like to get this finished as soon as possible." He shrugged his shoulders and changed the subject. "I have special instructions concerning one of your prisoners, if he is still alive."

"Which one, sir?"

"The prophet—" Nebuzaradan glanced at a scroll he carried to make sure of the name—"Jeremiah. Nebuchadnezzar has granted this man his freedom."

"Is that so? He's helped to calm the fearful and keep them

in order. I'll be sorry to lose him."

"You might not lose him."

"How's that?" The guard looked puzzled.

"He has permission to live in Babylon if he chooses."

"Well, let's see what he wants to do." The warden turned to an aide and said, "Fetch Jeremiah for me."

The aide was gone only a few minutes before he returned with a tall, thin man who had kind but piercing eyes framed by white hair and beard.

"Are you Jeremiah?" Nebuzaradan asked.

"Yes, sir."

"The Great King, King Nebuchadnezzar of Babylon," the captain spoke slowly and used the correct protocol for speaking of the king in the presence of a conquered slave, "is pleased to grant you your freedom."

Nebuzaradan thought he had never seen a face so radiant with peace, yet this man had spent two years in prison—caged by his own people because he had tried to save them from this tragedy. *What a man!* the captain thought to himself. *If he had been king instead of Zedekiah, his people would still inhabit their city.* "You are no longer a prisoner," he continued.

"Thank you, sir," Jeremiah answered with a bow. "But why should I be treated so kindly? I am but a poor slave."

"More like a hero, I'd say. The Great King, King Nebuchadnezzar of Babylon, knows how you urged Zedekiah to remain loyal and all the indignities you suffered because of your efforts. If all your people had served Yahweh like you and Daniel do, this whole sad affair would never have happened."

"I've only done my duty, sir. I ask no favors."

"But you shall have them." The captain paused to read from his scroll. "The Great King, King Nebuchadnezzar of Babylon, commands me to set you free. You may go with me to Babylon, where I will supply you with a house of your own and plenty of food and clothing for the rest of your life. Or, if you choose, you may remain here in Judah. I don't advise that, however, because the country lies waste, and few houses still stand. But you may stay if you wish."

The Babylonian officer thought for a moment. "If you do decide to stay with Gedaliah son of Ahikam in Mizpah. My master has appointed him ruler over your people."

"You are kind indeed, sir." Again Jeremiah bowed. "I knew Gedaliah's father, Ahikam, and I feel safe in his hands."

"Very well, then." Nebuzaradan handed Jeremiah a small sack filled with heavy objects. "This gift from the Great King, King Nebuchadnezzar of Babylon, contains enough money to supply your needs for many months to come. Can I serve you in any other way?"

"Yes, sir, if it please you, sir." Jeremiah bowed a third time. "I have two friends among the captives. I beg of you that they might accompany me."

"Who are they?"

"Baruch, my scribe, and Ebed-Melech, Zedekiah's eunuch."

"Ah yes, the man who saved your life." Nebuzaradan turned to the guard. "Do you have these men?"

"Yes, sir." The guard frowned. "They, too, are model prisoners, sir. You are taking the ones who help keep the rest under control."

"Never mind. You have enough men to handle the prisoners. Now get Baruch and Ebed-Melech for me."

Jeremiah embraced his friends when they arrived, and every eye filled with tears. Even Nebuzaradan felt somehow touched by the tender scene.

"I will also give these men money for the journey," the captain said. "May Yahweh, your God, continue to bless you as He has in the past."

"And may Yahweh bless you and his majesty, King

Nebuchadnezzar," Jeremiah returned.

The three men strolled down the road toward Mizpah, only two miles northwest, as they shared with each other the experiences of the past month. At the top of a hill they turned for a last look at the prison camp. They stared for several minutes, each lost in his thoughts.

Finally Jeremiah broke the stillness. "Thanks be to Yahweh." He turned toward Mizpah. "We're free at last."

Epilogue

Jeremiah's life after his release remained as complicated as before. He lived in Mizpah for only three months when Ishmael, a fanatical Judahite leader, rallied 10 men to help him take over the government. Besides slaughtering the Babylonian garrison, they murdered Gedaliah, his officials, and 70 other important men before herding the remainder of Mizpah's population toward Ammon—including Jeremiah, Baruch, and Ebed-Melech. Ishmael also took Zedekiah's wives and daughters for himself because by marrying these women he thought he could make himself king.

But all his plans failed. A Judahite general named Johanan attacked him at Gibeon and rescued all the people. Ishmael, however, managed to escape to Ammon with eight of his men.

Johanan feared that Nebuchadnezzar would interpret Ishmael's uprising as rebellion and return to deport the remnant of the land's native population. Jeremiah encouraged him to remain in Judah. "Nebuchadnezzar won't harm you," he said, "but if you take the people off to Egypt, the Babylonians will destroy you."

Paying him no attention, Johanan forced nearly the entire local population to march to Egypt, leaving Judah virtually deserted. He settled his captives in Tahpanhes, where the Pharaoh maintained a palace, and before long the Jews fell to worshipping the Egyptian gods.

Some years later Nebuchadnezzar invaded Egypt, defeated Pharaoh in a pitched battle, captured Tahpanhes, killed most of the Jewish men, and brought the survivors to Babylon in chains.

History does not reveal the exact circumstances of Jeremiah's death, although three conflicting Jewish traditions give us some clues. One story reports that the Jews stoned him in Egypt because he preached against their false gods. A second claims that Nebuchadnezzar rescued him and convinced him to live out his remaining years in Babylon. The third tale suggests that Nebuchadnezzar allowed him to return to Judah, where he died of natural causes.

Baruch had hoped to rise in Jerusalem's royal bureaucracy, only to give up his dream and follow Jeremiah instead. But he earned fame after his death. He has become one of the few people in the Bible known to be mentioned on ancient artifacts. A seal found in Palestine bears the label "Belonging to Berechiah. Son of Neriah, the scribe." Berechiah is the long form of the name Baruch. Baruch also became a prominent figure in later Jewish tradition. Several pseudepigraphic works were composed under his name.

Zedekiah refused to follow Jeremiah's counsel because he thought he saw a contradiction between the predictions of Ezekiel and Jeremiah. Jeremiah wrote that Zedekiah would die as a captive in Babylon, while Ezekiel predicted that he would never see that city. The king grasped at this apparent disagreement as proof that both men were false prophets, even though they agreed on every other point. It never occurred to the king that both men could be right. He was blinded before his trip to Babylon, so he never actually saw the city. Nebuchanezar kept the king in a Babylonian dungeon until he died, then gave him a magnificient funeral.

The Babylonian ruler marveled at the faith of Jeremiah, Daniel, Shadrach, Meshach, and Abednego. No doubt their righteous lives convicted the pagan monarch that Yahweh was the only true God. But the treacherous conduct of other

Jews must have caused him no end of confusion. Consider the dishonest dealings and the vacillation of such kings as Jehoiakim and Zedekiah, and false prophets such as Hananiah in Judah and Ahab and Zedekiah in Babylon.

Nebuchadnezzar's treatment of Jeremiah reveals that the great Babylonian king respected him as a man of God, and some have suggested that he invaded Egypt partially for the purpose of rescuing the aging prophet.

The Babylonian ruler himself lived a remarkable life. Toward its close he realized that he had been blessed by Yahweh, and after his last spiritual rebellion, he finally gave his heart to his Creator. He died a converted follower of the true God.

Author's Note

The last days of Judah as recorded in Jeremiah, though gruesome in detail, nevertheless provide us with a faithful warning of what could become of any Christian in the day of judgment if he or she were to stray from the pathway marked out in Scriptures. How appropriate, then, that all Christians study the fall of Judah and the messages that God sent to His people just prior to pouring out His judgments upon them.

But the book of Jeremiah often confuses readers because the text is not in chronological order. Reading the book in the sequence shown below will allow the narrative and the prophetic messages to unfold in the same order in which they occurred.

Events that happened during the reign of King Josiah (639-608 B.C.): Chapters 1-6; 14-16.

Events that happened during the reign of King Jehoiakim (608-597 B.C.): Chapters 17; 7-11; 26; 35; 22:1-19; 25; 18-20; 36:1-4; 45; 36:5-32; 12.

Events that happened during the reign of King Jehoiachin (597 B.C.): Chapters 22:20-30; 13; 23.

Events that happened during the reign of King Zedekiah (597-586 B.C.): Chapters 24; 29-31; 46-51; 27; 28; 21; 34; 32; 37; 33; 38; 39.

Events that happened after the fall of Jerusalem (after 586 B.C.): Chapters 40-44; 52.